North of South Haven

Praise for *North of South Haven*

North of South Haven is a tender, expansive novel about the long way home and the people who meet us there. … What unfolds is not just memory but rediscovery—delivered with humor, heartbreak, and unconditional love.

This is a story about how the landscape of our youth can both wound and repair us; how an act of kindness can reroute a life; and how, even in our most broken moments, we may stumble into a version of home that fits better than the one we left behind. Anchored in place and written with a keen eye for the small gestures that change everything, *North of South Haven* reminds us that the world often offers second chances. We just have to be brave enough to turn toward them.

—Doug Stanton, New York Times bestselling author of *In Harm's Way: The Sinking of the USS Indianapolis and the Extraordinary Story of Its Survivors and Horse Soldiers*

North of South Haven is a glass of lemonade on a hot summer day—sweet, satisfying, and delicious! I adored this charming story of heartbreak and hope, shattered dreams, and new beginnings. In a world of uncertainty, *North of South Haven* takes its reader to a quieter, gentler place where hearts mend, dreams blossom, and friends become family.

—Lori Nelson Spielman, international bestselling author of the *The Life List*

North of South Haven is a story about North Cooper, a woman who must face upheaval and healing when she receives life-changing news from her husband. *North of South Haven* explores the emotional journey through moments of sadness to calm feelings of peace. This novel dives into the relationships between North and the people she knows and loves. As a bonus, it is also set against the backdrop of beloved Michigan cities and the comfort of good food and local wines.

This book is for readers who have had to navigate the emotional toll from the complexities of marriage and understand that the end of something can sometimes lead to beautiful things.

—Holly Mayes, author of *Dream, Girl* and the Gem series

North of South Haven

Dayna Marie Edwards

and

Rob Edwards

Dayna Marie

M·P·P
www.MissionPointPress.com

This is a work of fiction. Names, places, and incidents are the products of the author's imagination or are used fictitiously. Any resemblance to actual events or locales or persons, living or dead, is entirely coincidental.

Mission Point Press
Published by Mission Point Press
MissionPointPress.com

Hardcover ISBN: 978-1-968761-35-6
Softcover ISBN: 978-1-968761-36-3
Library of Congress Control Number: Available upon request
Printed in the United States of America

By and for Dayna Marie 1966-2024

Forever loved.

Forever missed.

Chapter One

West.

Her car was moving much too fast down the two-lane highway, and all North Cooper knew was the direction she was heading.

Her heart had not just been broken; it had been shattered. Everything she believed to be true had been turned upside down. The blueprint of her life that she'd worked so many years to design, had been ripped into tiny pieces and tossed to the wind. So, she hopped into her car and picked a direction.

West.

Or maybe she didn't pick the direction, maybe it was the sandy shores of Lake Michigan that whispered to her—calling her to come back. In the past, whenever she'd felt overwhelmed or her anxiety became too much to bear, North would escape to the sunset side of Michigan, wade into the unsalted waters of the majestic lake, and let the stress drift off into the current. Then she would lie on a blanket in the sand, listen to the waves lapping against the shore and feel her soul calm down. She needed that now more than at any point in her life.

In the past she'd headed to typical high-end destination towns like Saugatuck, Holland, or Grand Haven. They were places she and her husband, Matthew, would go for long weekends or quick romantic get-aways. But heading to those places now would feel like returning to the scene of a crime.

The highway's gentle curves wound around blueberry farms and horse ranches, now and then there were gas stations with Subway sandwich shops inside, and oddly placed Dollar Stores.

For what seemed like the hundredth time, her phone played "Wind Beneath My Wings," by Bette Midler. It was Matthew's favorite song and what they danced to at their wedding. She would now have to change that ring tone. Perhaps "Lies" by the Thompson Twins was more fitting.

North didn't answer it—again. She didn't need to hear anything more from him. He'd said enough.

She knew he was worried about her. Her departure had been rushed and emotional, but what could he possibly expect? When the song started once again, she felt a twinge of guilt for what she was putting him through. She could easily pick up the phone, tell him she was fine and go live his new life, but she couldn't bring herself to do it. The guilt was there, yes, but so was a small, sharp satisfaction in letting him worry. It felt good to know that he had some concern for her. It was at least small validation that the entire seven years of their marriage hadn't been a total lie.

North pressed on the accelerator of her Subaru Imprezza, blurring the trees that swished by her car windows. When she rounded the next curve, she saw three does meandering across the road. She slammed on the brakes and the tires screamed against the pavement leaving black streaks and smoke behind her. Her purse and her quickly packed overnight bag tumbled to the floor of the passenger's side. She stopped just three feet short of the closest deer.

The does glanced at her lazily, flicking their ears and tails.

With her heart pounding, and her hands shaking, North snarled. How dare they look so unfazed after nearly killing her. "Get out of the road!" she shouted, leaning on the horn.

The deer startled, turned back, bumping into each other as they scrambled and bound back into the woods.

North took her hand off the horn and watched their white tails disappear into the green overgrowth. "I'm sorry," she whispered, and wiped away a tear. Strangely there was no satisfaction in disrupting Mother Nature's creatures, even if they disrupted her life first.

She looked into the rear-view mirror to make sure there was nobody behind her, took a deep breath, and put her foot back on the gas pedal. She drove slower now, scanning both sides of the road for any more creatures that may dart in front of her.

Soon she passed over an expressway and saw the sign announcing that South Haven lay straight ahead. Excitement flickered through her angst.

The speed limit slowed as the traffic thickened and her eyes shot back and forth for anything that looked familiar. She hadn't been to South Haven since her parents moved away when she was in fourth grade, but she felt that some things should still be the same.

She saw the sign for Phoenix Street and gasped. That was the road that would take her 25 years back in time. She swerved into the left turn lane. A car behind her honked. She looked in her rear-view mirror and waved apologetically. "Sorry."

When the light changed, North turned, and the quaint town of South Haven, Michigan welcomed her in. There was the cute little park on the left, where she used to sit with her dad and eat ice cream in the summertime. During holidays, she'd waited in line outside Santa's shack, trembling more from excitement than cold as she waited for her turn to sit on Santa's lap and tell him everything she wanted for Christmas.

She passed the island in the middle of the street that held the "Welcome to South Haven" sign, with its seagull art and silhouette of the iconic lighthouse. She continued down through the heart of the small lakeside village. The layout of the town was the same, but most all the places that she remembered from her childhood were gone. There were new signs, replacements for the businesses that were there before them.

But then her eyes caught Clementine's, where she used to go on Sundays with her parents to eat comfort food. North took a deep breath. This street brought back the feelings of a time when the world was a good place, when things were less complicated, and when she wasn't in any danger of being heartbroken.

On the other side of the charming downtown, Phoenix Street changed to Water Street that ran parallel with the mouth of the Black River which fed into Lake Michigan. It was landscaped now with a sidewalk, benches and stairs, but North remembered when her parents pulled their car off the road by the river and she would watch the fourth of July fireworks while eating sweet black cherries that they had picked from a local orchard earlier in the day, and spit the seeds into the water.

She passed a mostly empty municipal marina, and the far side of the river was lined with docks and boat slips that were also mostly empty because it was still early May. But after Memorial Day both sides would be filled, and the river would be jammed with sailboats, sport fishing boats, and yachts heading in both directions.

The road ended at a long pier stretching into Lake Michigan and North's heart leapt when she saw the bright red lighthouse, the symbol of South Haven, that let all passersby, on land and water, know they had arrived.

She drove around the corner and parked in the beach parking lot next to a small playground, where two young moms sat at picnic tables, in deep conversation, unconcerned that their children were walking the wrong way up the slide.

North got out of her car, staring at the lighthouse. She walked toward it as if she were in a trance and the lighthouse was the talisman that controlled her. When she reached the beach, she took off her blue Rothys and stepped out into the South Haven sand for the first time in over two decades. It was cold on her bare feet, but it somehow felt safe. Known.

She headed straight for the water which casually lapped up on the shore. She cried out when she reached the frigid water, remembering what it felt like to step into Lake Michigan just after it recovered from its winter freeze.

She wished she could remain there a little longer, but she didn't need frostbite along with the rest of her pain. Stepping back several yards, North sat in the cool soft sand, closed her eyes and let the breeze blow through her sandy blond hair. She listened as the waves broke, and the seagulls screeched at each other. Off to her left the children shouted and laughed, now jumping out of swings in midair. The air smelled fresh and clean, just like she remembered, except those quick seconds when the pungent odor of fish blew past.

For this brief moment in time North was calm. Contented even. She forgot momentarily her shattered heart. Tears weren't waiting to burst out, and she didn't want to curl up into a ball and die. She just wanted to listen to the waves, breathe in the crystal clean air, and think about the only time in her life when she was truly happy.

Her phone chimed in her purse, interrupting her happy trance. She pulled it out to see it was a text from Emma, her closest friend, who also happened to be her sister-in-law.

"Hey sister, Matt just called. He wanted to know if I'd talked to you. I'm so so so sorry. Please call me. We're all very worried about you. I love you and want to be there for you."

Matt's sister Emma was one of the sweetest people in North's life. They hit it off right away, and Emma was actually one of the deciding factors why she married Matt.

North didn't want to call her. She didn't want to talk to anybody, couldn't bring herself to speak or she would break down completely, and she didn't want to do that in public. She sent a text that contained only a broken heart emoji.

Not more than three seconds later her phone belted out the lyrics, "All I need in this life of sin is me and my girlfriend. Down to ride till the happy end, is me and my girlfriend." It was a song from Icona Pop, an obscure Swedish band, but it was North's and Emma's theme song, which was why North made it Emma's ring tone on her phone.

If she would have let it play out, she would have heard the verse, "Talking 'bout the lights, the dirt, the shit, that hurts." There had never been shit in North's life that hurt as bad as this, but she couldn't talk now, to Emma or anybody. With a quick swish of her thumb she declined the call.

Her phone chimed again. This time it was a text from Matt. "I see from your GPS that you're over in South Haven. Please let me know you're all right. I'm sorry. I do love you."

North gritted her teeth and felt her whole body tense. She could not hear that from him, nor did she believe it. And it angered her that he had the ability to check up on her and know her location. He no longer had that right. She would have to figure out how to turn that feature off, but she could fix it immediately by hitting the power button. It was becoming a tedious interruption anyway. She came this far to escape everything, not deal with it at a distance.

She slipped the phone back into her purse and closed her eyes again, but the calm moment had passed. The cool breeze now just felt bitter cold, and it seemed to smell too much like fish. She could no longer relax so she stood and brushed off the sand. North knew what would make everything better on a day like today. She needed a fresh, warm donut and a glass of chocolate milk. She remembered there was a bakery up the street where her dad used to take her whenever she was feeling blue. It was always the perfect medicine.

Walking up the sidewalk along the Black River, North couldn't believe how much everything had changed. First of all, it was much more attractive and easier for tourists to navigate. She had to admit it was beautiful with well-manicured lawns, smartly trimmed bushes, and flower beds of lavender, petunias, and black-eyed Susans. But North didn't like it. There was nothing wrong with the way the riverfront used to be—a little wild with crab grass and clover. But now if a car were to pull up next to the river, the driver would have to jump the curb and drive over the flowers, which would likely get them arrested. The beautifying of the town of her youth just felt like one more thing that was taken from her. North sighed.

A fishing boat was coming down the Black River fitted with long outriggers on the back and downriggers on the side. The two gentlemen on board were serious about their fishing. One was inside the cabin steering, but the other was standing on the back deck holding a beer. They both waved at North. She waved back because it was the unwritten rule of the Great Lakes. If a boat passes you, both parties are required to wave. At least that hadn't changed.

It was early May, so tourist season hadn't really kicked in yet. The sidewalks were empty, but the restaurants were optimistically open. North smelled a savory whiff coming from a restaurant known as Captain Nemos, but savory wasn't what she was in the mood for. Savory never helped one single heartbreak in all of history.

A mother came toward her holding the hands of twin boys crying because they wanted fudge from the Kilwin's Fudge store and she had to tell them no. Then they passed another little store called Harbor

Toys that had brightly colored balls, stuffed animals, and spinning pinwheels out front. Both boys pulled on their mother's hands to go in, but she held their hands tightly and walked by, which wasn't well received by her children. They both started an ear-piercing wailing. The mother rolled her eyes, then glanced over at North, shaking her head with a look that said she was sorry.

North passed a few more storefronts and stopped, puzzled. She looked up and down the street but could not find her bakery. How could it not be here? It was a South Haven staple. Maybe whoever said 'you can't ever go home again' was right.

Walking toward the end of the block she saw the red ceramic-colored building of Clementine's across the street. If she couldn't get a freshly baked donut, perhaps she could get a fresh stack of pancakes. Crossing the street a small black flag waving in the breeze caught her attention. It had one word in white letters, "Coffee." Perhaps that would hit the spot.

She neared the coffee shop and was quickly overtaken by the soothing smell of freshly brewed coffee. It said WE above the door, but Water's Edge on the window. She entered to find that the place had an "old college town" kind of feel. It was rustic with exposed brick walls, plush chairs positioned around an old wooden coffee table, (what else) in the center, booths off to one side and a counter with stools at the window facing the street. It was as if someone transplanted a coffee shop from Ann Arbor into her old hometown.

North ordered a hot chocolate and a blueberry muffin from an extremely friendly woman whose nametag read "Margie." Muffin in hand, she stepped aside while her hot chocolate was being prepared. Glancing around the quaint space she saw a handful of people taking casual sips of their coffee while working on laptops or scrolling through their phones. Two women in jeans and windbreakers, sat on the couch, cups in hand, facing each other, lost in conversation. The entire room was cozy and content. That was North's life yesterday. It's funny how quickly things can change.

A young barista with her long red hair pulled back into a ponytail sat a cup on the counter. "Hot chocolate, whipped cream."

"Thank you," North took her warm cup, grabbed a couple of napkins and sat in a booth. She looked at the muffin and realized how hungry she was. She hadn't eaten much of her lunch before she rushed out of the restaurant.

North took a bite of the soft, crumbly muffin and a quick drink of the hot chocolate. She closed her eyes and let the sweet flavors soothe her, doing her best to be as content as the other people in the room. She tried to focus on the moment and not the swirling mess her life had turned into. North was here, in a delightful little coffee shop, eating her blueberry muffin and drinking a delicious cup of hot chocolate, and she had nothing but a beautiful spring day next to Lake Michigan to look forward to.

The door opened behind her, and a loud, piercing voice cut through her reverie. "It's been a day already, and I need a cookie."

North's eyes snapped open. She knew that voice. It was from her past.

The woman behind the counter chuckled. "What can I get you, El?"

"I'll take one of those, chocolate chip yummies, please."

"Sure thing," the woman said.

North spun around to see an African American woman standing in front of the counter, her arms folded, with a small leather purse hanging off one arm. Her hair, braided, was up on her head and mostly gray. That was not how North remembered her. Though the face was older now, wrinkled around the eyes and sagging in the cheeks, the woman was unmistakably..."Aunt El?"

Chapter Two

Eljerita Jones looked sideways at North, her eyes scanning up and down while the gears in her head were clicking away trying to figure out what white girl could possibly call her aunt.

The woman wasn't really North's aunt. She had lived next door to North's family and became a very close friend—so close, in fact, that she was given the honorary title of Aunt to North. She had always acted like an aunt too, often showing much more love and kindness to North than her own mother did.

It didn't take long for El to connect all the pieces. Her expression changed from one of confusion to one of delight. She put her hands on her hips and screamed, "North Nichols?" Then she opened her arms wide. "My goodness girl, get over here!"

North jumped up from her table and rushed into the waiting arms of someone she knew loved her—or at least, who did at one point in her life.

Aunt El was still strong and her arms wrapped around North, bear-hug style, and held on tight while her laughter rang out like music to North's lonely ears. She chuckled happily. She was soft and warm as a chenille blanket on a cold winter's night, and she smelled like cherries and vanilla. Then she pulled back and gripped North's shoulders, holding her at arm's length. "Let me look at you." El shook her head and smiled. "You're all grown up and look beautiful."

It was beginning to feel a little weird for North now. She had been all grown up for several years and El was talking to her like she was fifteen instead of thirty-two.

El finally released her and turned to the woman behind the counter. "Margie, I'll take a coffee too. I need to spend some time with my little girl here." She shooed North away with her hand. "Go sit down, sweetie. I'll be right over and I want to hear everything about everything."

North took her seat wondering what she had opened up. It was definitely a treat to see Aunt El again after all these years, but she wasn't sure she could talk about her life at the moment. She was *running* from her life. All she wanted to do was bury herself in her muffin and hot chocolate experience.

Aunt El dropped into the booth across from her and looked at North gleefully. "I had no idea when I woke up this morning that I would run into you, of all people. This day just became the greatest."

North smiled and looked down at her muffin. She had to admit, it felt good having someone be so happy to see her. She couldn't remember the last time this happened. Perhaps she *would* try to talk to Aunt El. At least she felt she would get the support she needed.

El opened a napkin and laid it out in front of her like a placemat. Then she carefully unwrapped her cupcake, pulled the bottom off and stuck it on the top, sandwiching the chocolate icing in the center. "Just spreading the wealth," El said with a wink. Then she bit into it. It was the most ingenious way North had ever seen anyone eat a cupcake, and she knew she would now eat them that way from this moment forward.

El washed down her bite with a cup of coffee. "Okay, tell me everything that's been going on with you, and don't leave anything out."

North opened her mouth to speak, but nothing came out. How should she begin? What could she say to this woman who hadn't seen her in years? How do you admit that your life has been one bad decision after another, culminating in the worst heartbreak of your life? Tears welled up in her eyes and all she managed to do was cry, the exact thing she was trying not to do.

"Oh, my goodness." El placed her cupcake on her placemat, wiped her mouth with another napkin, then reached out and squeezed North's hand. "It's alright. Aunt El is here now. We're doing this together."

Tears dropped into her hot chocolate and North moved the mug away. She did her best to stop crying, but the tears only increased, like snow melt in the spring. She tightened her grip on Aunt El's hand. The touch felt good—comforting somehow—like there was love flowing from one hand into the other.

The woman named Margie quietly dropped a large pile of napkins on the edge of the table and walked away.

"Thank you, dear," Aunt El said. She picked up a couple and handed them to North.

Hating to release her hands, North let go, took the napkins and blew her nose, then crumpled them up and dabbed at her eyes, trying to wipe at the mascara that was surely running down her face.

"When you're ready, I want to hear all about it," Aunt El said, with a gentleness in her voice. The sound of excitement was gone. All she had was genuine concern and caring for North. The thought that there was still someone out there who loved her made her cry even harder.

After a few minutes, the raging waters had slowed and North was able to compose herself. She blew her nose with more napkins and wiped at her face. "How do I look?" she asked Aunt El. "Do I have make-up everywhere?"

"Like a picture, love," Aunt El said, with a warm smile. She reached over and took North's hand again. "Tell me about this man who hurt you so bad."

"He's not just a man," North said. "He's my husband."

"So, your husband had an affair?" Aunt El nodded as she put the pieces together. "And you just found out about it. You came running home to South Haven to get away from it all."

The flow of tears began again, and North nodded as she wiped them away.

"That dirty piece of slime." Aunt El took North's hand again. "I'm here, girl. Tell me all about it."

North collected herself again and slowly began talking about her life with Matthew. He had been in medical school at the University of Michigan and she an interior design student at Washtenaw Community College—her third degree-program—when they had met at a mutual friend's summer cookout. They had been inseparable from that day forward.

She had gone with Matt while he completed his residency and fellowship at Boston General before he had proposed to her during a swan boat ride in the Public Garden. They were married in the Old North Church, the same church that hung two lanterns letting Paul Revere know the British were coming by sea.

Matthew and North had always loved each other very much, but their intimacy waned. North had assumed it was because of the long hours and all of the stress associated with being a doctor. After his residency, Matt was hired by the University of Michigan Hospital, and the two of them settled back in Ann Arbor to get their real life started. Matthew was a well-respected cardiac specialist and North, who had yet to finish a degree, was keeping quite busy doing a great deal of volunteer work with the Washtenaw Humane Society, the U of M Hospital, and as a newsreader for the visually impaired through Michigan Radio.

In the past four years, they had made it to London, Paris, and Rome. They were certainly going to travel more, but they'd made the decision, while riding a swan boat in Boston, that the first places they would visit across the pond were the "big three." It was another goal they had achieved together, and North and Matthew seemed like an unstoppable couple.

Together, they had made the decision that kids would be their next big step. Four was the number, two boys and two girls (as if you get to choose that), and North had even started preparing all of the rooms. Being very organized, she wanted to have everything ready before she became pregnant.

But it never happened. The timeline for having kids kept getting diverted and delayed.

In the past couple of years, their storybook life had grown cracks. Matthew was working constantly and became very irritable, so North had tried to do things to ease his stress; she made his favorite meals, scratched his head (which always calmed him down), and surprised him with little weekend getaways.

Eventually, Matt was working so much, he was not coming home for his favorite meals, scratching his head only seemed to be an irritant, and the special weekends were canceled at the last minute.

"I'll be honest," North said. "I was that wife who began pushing the 'baby' thing really hard because I thought it was the only way to save the marriage." She shook her head and wiped at another tear. "But there wasn't anything that would have saved our marriage. It was doomed from the very beginning."

"Why do you say that, sweetie?"

North looked into the eyes of Aunt El, and saw so much concern and kindness in them. This woman, whom she hadn't seen in decades, was willing to pick up right where they left off: being the motherly stand-in when her own mother was too self-absorbed to care. In truth, Aunt El had been the only soft place for North in her entire life. Running into her now, on this—the worst day of her life—seemed truly a gift from a higher power.

The woman scowled and nodded at her. "Because 'Doc' Matt got all about himself and couldn't keep his johnny in its cage. He had to show it to all of the nurses, didn't he?"

North laughed. She even surprised herself by the sound of it. But she couldn't help herself. This beautiful woman across from her, one of the few to ever really care about her, was so loving and fiercely loyal that she was now ready to tear North's husband apart to protect her.

North shook her head. "No, it's not quite like that." North picked up her mug of hot chocolate and swirled the last little bit around in the bottom. "It's not a nurse. *He's* another doctor."

Chapter Three

"Wait." Aunt El sat back in her seat and scrunched her brows together. "Did you say … '*he*?'"

North nodded.

"So, you're telling me you married a man who was gay?"

"I guess so," North sighed. "But I didn't know it at the time."

"You couldn't tell?"

"No." North found herself irritated at the question. "How could I tell? He said he loved me. We did so much together, we were inseparable. And to be honest, the sex was … you know … amazing."

Aunt El sat back and took a slow sip of her coffee. Then she set it back down on the table and looked at North with the same stern expression a detective might have when grilling a suspect. "All this time *he* didn't know he was gay?"

North shrugged. "He says he didn't. He said it was this relationship that opened up that part of his heart, and now it's not something he can close off and let go."

Aunt El reached over, patted North's hand, and took it while gently rubbing the back of it with her thumb. "Sweetie, I know this may hurt … but I'm not sure getting angry at a person for not knowing who they really are inside is … good for *you*."

"I didn't say I was angry at *him*," North said. "I'm angry at myself for not seeing it. I'm angry at myself for not being prepared for something like this, and I'm so sad at losing the dream of our life together as a couple." Tears welled up in North's eyes once more; an endless supply of salty bitter tears that wouldn't stop running. "All our dreams … just … gone." She flitted her hand in the air.

The door to the coffee shop opened and a woman walked in with three young children, who noisily ran over to the display case and put their hands and faces all over it, longingly looking at the delicious pastries.

Aunt El patted North's hand and shook it firmly. "Okay, deary, let's get you out of here."

"I've got no place to go," North said, trying to hold back her grief so she didn't break down in front of the children.

"But you do," Aunt El said. "You're going to stay with me until we get all this figured out. You can have Lilly's room."

North remembered Lilly Jones. She was several years older and had been much too cool at the time to be seen with her—as any true big sister would.

Aunt El stood and waved at North to get up. "Come on. Tears and hot chocolate time is over. Let's get some fresh air." She grabbed North's mug and placed it into a bussing bin.

North slowly crumpled up her napkin, and somehow found the energy to slide herself out of the booth seat and stand.

"Come on, sweetie." Aunt El took her hand and walked her toward the door.

North threw her napkin in the trash on the way out.

The brisk spring air hit North like a splash of cold water on the face. She stepped back, gasped, and shook her head.

"Wakes you up, doesn't it?" El said.

It did wake her up. North suddenly realized she was completely lost. She had no real skills, no college degree, and no natural direction in her life. Honestly, she wasn't even emotionally equipped right now to find one. She was suddenly so overwhelmed with fear and dismay that she couldn't force herself to take another step.

"Where's your car?" El said, gently tugging at her hand.

North stood rooted on the sidewalk, staring directly ahead, yet seeing nothing. Her mind raced, searching for answers to her situation and finding none. Her shoulders slumped and her arms hung limp, realizing she was now in real trouble.

Aunt El placed her hands lightly on North's shoulders. "Come on, child. Let's get you someplace where you can properly have a breakdown. My car is right over here," she coaxed.

North felt El nudge her forward and managed to get her feet to move in that direction. El guided her to a white Range Rover that was parked at an angle in front of the coffee shop. El opened the door and North slid into the seat.

The inside of the car was immaculate and the aroma of cherries and vanilla was much stronger. A thin metal symbol that looked like a flower with four petals hung from the rearview mirror, with a tassel of red and green threads streaming below it. It was a striking piece and North couldn't take her eyes off it, as it jiggled and swung while El got in the car on the driver's side. She pointed at it. "That's very pretty."

Aunt El started the car. "That's Nsirewa. It's the African Adinkra symbol that stands for unity, togetherness, and harmony."

"It actually means something?" North asked. She reached up and held it in her hands, examining the four petals more closely. They were symmetrical, stretching in all four directions with a line running halfway through each petal. It was made of tin, which was discolored and dingy with age. "Nsirewa," North said, to try to put the word and its meaning into her head. She lowered her hand from the metal piece and let the thin strands of the tassel slide through her fingers. "I think I like it even more now."

"Mm hmm." El nodded, backing the car from its parking spot. "It's nice, isn't it?" She put the car into drive and headed down the street. "We'll come back for your car after you've had time to collect yourself."

El turned onto Kalamazoo Street and headed into the quaint neighborhoods that surrounded the downtown area. North watched the crackerbox and two-story homes go by, thinking they looked like the cliché of a small American town: beautifully manicured lawns with white picket fences; small brick walkways leading up to front doors lined with flower beds where tulips and petunias would soon be blooming; and brightly painted homes in pastel greens, blues, even pinks, with ornately painted porches glittering with a variety of wind chimes. There were proud homeowners, here and there, out raking up the stray leaves from the fall and getting ready for the new growth of spring, but for the most part, the neighborhoods were still very quiet. North knew that in just a few weeks, these streets would be bustling with life, with cars, bikers, and foot traffic heading in every direction.

El turned down another street, and North realized that everything seemed very familiar all of a sudden. She pulled into the driveway of a small, light blue ranch with trim painted white.

"Here we are," El said, stopping the car in front of a tiny detached garage.

"This is your house," North said, recognizing it.

"I know," El said, turning off the car and pulling the keys from the ignition. "I told you I was bringing you here."

"You still live here." North looked at the house which was now a different color—it used to be green.

"I do." El opened her car door. "For forty-two years now. Come on, let's get you situated." She stood and closed the door.

North got out and looked at the house next door. It was also a different color, having been a bright butter-yellow when she was a little girl. It now had tan vinyl siding, but it still had the same gray cement steps leading up to the side door. Those were the same steps that North had slipped on one cold wintry morning, fallen, and broken her left arm. They were also the same steps she had stood on as a little girl, shivering in the rain, because she had walked home from school in first grade, and her mother wouldn't let her in. "If you want to be independent, go be independent," she had said. It was Aunt El who had seen her sitting out there, soaked, brought her inside, wrapped her in warm blankets in front of the TV, and given her tomato soup in a cup. North's mother had come by later and acted surprised that North was there, saying she didn't hear her knocking. Aunt El had said that North was no bother, but North had always wondered if Aunt El knew what was really going on.

"Come on inside, honey." El said, pulling North back into the present decade. "I want to show you where you're going to be staying."

North looked back at the cement steps. It made sense now why she never brought Matthew here, and why she had never come back until now. Not every memory was idyllic. She turned and followed El up her own brick walkway, up the small wooden porch steps in front of her house, where a couple of white wooden rocking chairs and a wooden porch swing sat, and into the house.

Everything was different, yet still the same. The living room was now a peaceful sea-salt blue, instead of the dull beige it had been when North was a little girl. Under the window, where there had once stood a large entertainment system, was now an oversized chair and matching ottoman, and the black and orange plaid sofa was gone, replaced with a distressed brown leather one that now faced the brick fireplace. Above the mantle hung a large flat-screen television, angled down for better viewing from the sofa.

North walked over to the mantle to see an array of pictures lined up. There was Lilly, looking much older than North remembered her, in a graduation gown and cap in one, and a wedding gown in another. There were pictures of Lilly and El in Hawaii and in front of the Eiffel Tower. There were pictures of Lilly holding a baby, then pushing two in a stroller, and at the end were school pictures of two boys, smiling big for the camera. The smallest one had a front tooth missing.

"Lilly's married with a family?"

"Yes, she is," El said. "She went to Grand Valley after high school and became a nurse. She lives with her husband up in Rockford, just north of Grand Rapids and works at Butterworth."

"Good for her," North said. She wanted to truly be happy for Lilly, but these pictures just made her ache for what she didn't have and now wondered if she ever would.

"Let's get you into your room." North followed El down a hall. She stopped at a door that had a locked handle and a deadbolt on it. "This is Lilly's old room, but I've made some updates." El opened the door to reveal another door behind it. She jingled her set of keys until she found the right one, then opened the second door into the room. "I had the room redone and put it up for rent on Airbnb."

North walked into the room that used to be Lilly's but was now clean and bright with a coziness that is difficult to find in most standard hotel rooms.

El pointed to the opposite wall. "I had a door put in that leads to the backyard, so you don't have to come through the front door of the house to access the room."

The bedroom was light gray with white trim and contained a pine four-poster, queen-sized bed topped with multiple pillows and a thick white comforter. Two pine nightstands flanked either side of the bed with brass bedside lamps illuminating the room. Above the bed was a large framed photo of the iconic South Haven lighthouse, silhouetted against a sparkling sunset, and on the opposite wall was a modest flat-screen TV hanging above a small turquoise bureau. On it was a coffee maker and a small sign that read, "Relax and enjoy the Wi-Fi." Written in chalk next to the word "Network" was "ElNet," and next to the word "Password" was "Calvinis5!" A mini refrigerator was built into the bureau and stocked with a variety of beverages. A suitcase holder leaned folded against the wall next to it. Around the room hung small wooden signs with sayings like, "Go jump in the lake," and "Great Lakes, unsalted."

Next to the back door was a small bistro table with two tall chairs. On the table was a basket of granola bars, small packets of trail mix, and bite-sized Snickers bars. El pointed to an open doorway and giddily said, "I recently worked with a contractor and a plumbing company to add an en suite." She turned on the light in the small bathroom, which contained a pedestal sink, toilet, and shower. "Aunt El, this is amazing," North said. "But if I stay here, you won't be able to rent it out."

"There's nobody to rent it to right now," El said. "It's still the off-season, so you aren't costing me a thing." She walked over to a white louvered door next to the turquoise bureau and pulled it open. "And here's a small closet for … when you have something to put in it." She looked up at North and smiled. "And here's the coolest thing about this room." She pointed to a small hatch door next to the main doorway and slid it open to reveal a small counter. "This is where I put the tray of breakfast for the guests when they want to eat, but they're not wearing anything." She giggled, and let the door slide closed.

"Oh, the things I've heard coming out of this room. Sometimes I have to turn the TV up." She giggled again and walked out of the room. "Anyway, this room is yours until you don't need it anymore. I'm going to go pull it off-line right now so that it doesn't get rented until you figure things out."

"Aunt El, I can't ask you to do that." North followed her out.

"You're not asking anything of me," El said as she turned around to look North in the eye. "I'm doing it because my girl needs help, and I'll be damned if I'm not going to make sure she's taken care of."

That statement and the determined expression on El's face left North without words. Was it possible that someone actually loved her that much? The thought brought tears back to her eyes—not tears of sadness, but not tears of joy either. They were tears of contentment, safety … love.

"Oh, there, there, sweetie." Aunt El walked back in and wrapped her loving arms around North while she cried. "I've got you. You've got nothing to worry about." This time the hug didn't seem awkward. It seemed genuine. North reached up and held this woman—this gift—tightly, and soaked in as much of this positive energy as she could before collecting herself and letting go.

"Why don't you go lie down?" El said. "There's bottled water in the fridge. Get yourself a drink and some rest. I'll go make us a proper dinner. You'll get sick only eating muffins and hot chocolate."

She wasn't sure she could eat anything else, but North said nothing. She wandered back into the room that her long-lost Aunt El had supplied for her and looked around. Was this her world now? Did she just drive away from her $400,000 Ann Arbor home to live within these four tiny walls?

She opened the mini fridge inside the bureau to find six Aquafina bottles lined up in the door. She grabbed one, twisted off the cap, and took a drink. It wasn't until the bottle touched her lips that she truly realized how thirsty she was. She kept drinking, consuming over half of the bottle before lowering it and taking a breath.

Sitting down on the bed, North kicked off her Rothy's, laid back, and looked up at the popcorn texture of the ceiling. All was quiet now. Peaceful. The only sounds she could hear were birds outside her window and the clicks and clacks of Aunt El tinkering in the kitchen.

North thought again about what her next move should be. It was clear that Matthew wanted to pursue this other relationship, which meant she was going to be on her own. That was a frightening prospect for her. She had never really taken the time to become self-sufficient. She didn't think she would ever need to.

She realized she desperately needed to talk to Emma. Emma was her sister from another mister and the only real friend she had. She was her person and the one she always turned to, but she was also Matthew's little sister. Pulling her phone out of her purse, she powered it on. It buzzed several times in her hands while it loaded texts and voice mails. Matthew had left five messages. That meant he had called close to fifty times.

Emma had left three texts. The first one read, "So worried girlfriend. Please call," followed by, "My heart is breaking. Just want to talk to you." Then the last one, "North. Call me." North clicked on the phone icon and hit Emma's number. It rang once and then picked up. "Hey," Emma said, sounding strangely cold.

"Hi," North said, trying to contain herself, lest she start crying again.

"You safe?" There was a strange sound to Emma. She sounded agitated.

"Yes. I'm in South Haven a …"

"Good. Glad to hear you're safe."

North wasn't expecting such a cold reaction. This was her

sister-in-law and closest friend in the world. "Why do you sound like you're mad at me?"

"Oh, I don't know, perhaps because you ran off and didn't tell anyone where you're going." Emma was definitely charged up. "We have been worrying about you all day, thinking you ran your car into a tree, jumped off a bridge, or whatever."

"I'm sorry, Emm, I just ..."

"You're sorry? No. You're selfish." Emma's voice was now low and rumbly.

"Emma," North's voice cracked. "I'm dealing with a lot here. I would think you of all people ..."

"There you go. *You're* dealing with a lot. Well, what about Matthew?"

North could hardly speak. She hadn't expected such a harsh greeting from someone who swore non-judgment and unwavering loyalty to her on several occasions. She wanted to say, *you mean the man who lied to me for years about who he was, the man who is now turning his back on me? That man?* Instead, all she could do was squeak out, "What about him?"

"I just came from him, North. He's worried sick about you. He's shaking, and he can't stop crying."

North wanted to scream, *good!* She was incredulous at this reaction. "Emma, do you understand what's really going on here? This whole thing is shocking and inconceivably hard on me."

"Hard on *you*?" Emma was screaming now. "It's hard on *you*? How do you think it is for *him*? Are you really that insensitive, North? How hard do you think it would be to wake up one day and realize all the choices you've made were the wrong ones?"

North's eyes narrowed. She now had frost in her own voice. "It would appear that is *exactly* what I've done." There was silence on the other end. "I'm going to hang up now, Emma. Goodbye."

"Sure, you're going to hang up," Emma shouted. "You're gonna run because that's what …"

North turned off the call, stared at the phone in her hand, and saw she, too, was now shaking. Her best and last friend in this world had just turned on her so viciously. Now it was certain: she was all alone in this world. She had nowhere to turn and no one to turn to.

"Hey sweetie," El called from the kitchen. "I'll have dinner ready in five minutes. I hope you're okay with leftover lasagna and iceberg lettuce salad."

Chapter Four

North shut the door to the microwave and turned it on for five minutes. Cooking the cut potatoes in the microwave before finishing them in the pan was a secret she'd learned on a Food Network show. It sped up the preparation process, while ensuring a crisp finish. She stirred the onions that were caramelizing in the nonstick pan, then broke two eggs into a glass bowl and whisked them with a fork.

She was making her kind Aunt El her signature breakfast burritos—one of the things she made that Matthew had always loved. In fact, he often told her that she should get herself a food truck because she would make a fortune selling them at events.

North was wearing a blue and orange Chicago Bears t-shirt, torn in the front, obviously to highlight the previous owner's cleavage. El had found it crumpled in a corner after one of her guests had left. She had washed it and saved it for them in case they ever called and asked for it, but last night, she gave it to North to sleep in. Over it, North wore one of El's robes, which was covered with patterns of flowering vines—not North's style, but flowery patterns were always a favorite of El's.

"The house smells amazing," El said, shuffling out from her

bedroom. “Who said you could do any cooking here? I’m the one who’s supposed to be taking care of you.”

“You’re up,” North said. “You’ve done a great job taking care of me. I wanted to do something for you for a change.” North grabbed a mug and the coffeepot, turning to El, “How do you like your coffee?”

“My goodness,” El said. “You’ve got coffee made already? Black, please.”

North poured and set the mug of coffee down on the table where she had already laid a place setting. “Have a seat right here while I finish getting your breakfast ready.”

El sat, lifted the mug to her nose, and sniffed deeply. “I swear, nothing smells better in the morning than a fresh cup of coffee that someone else made for you.” She winked, then took a sip.

North chuckled. “I hope you enjoy your breakfast, too, because I’m trying to butter you up for a really big ask.”

“Oh?” El said, swallowing. “Well, let me tell you; you’re doing all the right things. Go ahead and ask.”

“Let me finish breakfast and we’ll talk.”

When the microwave went off, North pulled out a hot glass bowl of cut potatoes and poured them into a pan with sizzling onions, sausage, and jalapeños. After the cloud of steam cleared, she threw a pat of butter on top, seasoned it with kosher salt, cumin, and black pepper, and left the potatoes to caramelize.

In another pan, she poured the beaten eggs and whisked them into a scramble, adding a tablespoon of sour cream and a handful of grated sharp cheddar cheese.

Then, she threw two large tortillas into the microwave for twenty seconds, pulled them out, and started assembling her breakfast burritos. First, she placed the sliced avocado on the tortillas, dribbled salsa verde down the middle, added the potato hash, then topped it all with the cheesy eggs. She rolled them up perfectly, cut them in half at an angle, and placed them on plates with a modest helping of sliced cantaloupe. Then, she set the plate down, restaurant presentation style, in front of El.

"This looks like a picture in a cooking magazine," El said. "I don't know if I should eat it or put it on the mantle."

North laughed while she poured her own cup of coffee, grabbed her plate, and sat at the table. "I felt the same way about your lasagna last night."

El took a bite and closed her eyes. "Mmmmm." She washed it down with a sip of coffee. "This is absolutely heavenly. I need to hire you to cook breakfasts for my guests."

"Well, how about if I at least cook breakfasts for you while I'm staying here?" North asked.

"Deal," El chuckled, clinking her coffee cup with North's in agreement. She took another sip and set her cup back on the table. "So, what was the big ask?"

North had just taken a bite from her burrito, and held up a finger while she chewed. She swallowed and held her hand in front of her mouth while she spoke. "It became apparent to me yesterday, when I talked with Emma that I no longer have a future in Ann Arbor." She took a sip of coffee and washed her bite down. "I went to sleep feeling completely lost. My life is a certified disaster, and my future feels like I'm destined to live at the bottom of a deep, dark pit."

"Oh, honey," El said, shaking her head. "That's not …"

"No wait," North held up a hand. "But when I woke up this morning, the sun was shining through the window and the birds were singing outside. Everything was different. Instead of being crushed that everyone turned on me, I realized I was angry that everything was so

… fake. Not only was my husband dishonest with me, he wasn't being true to himself. And that's worse. He needs to get that figured out."

"That's right, he does," El said.

"But believe it or not, I'm over that …" She looked up at the ceiling. "Okay, I'm not over that, but I'm doing my damnedest to try to understand it. But Emma, I can't forgive. I mean, I understand family loyalty and all, but for the past eight years, I've been family, too. For her to just forget all that we've meant to each other just like that," she said, snapping her fingers, "I can't get past that. It means that she lied to me all those times she said we were sisters, that she loved me like a sister—all those things two closest friends say to each other. All of that was fake, and I can't understand it, let alone get past it."

"I hope, in time, you can," El said, her eyes sad, like those of a dachshund puppy.

North stuck her burrito back into her mouth and took a small bite.

"I still don't know what the big ask is," El said and took her own bite.

North held up a finger once more while she chewed. "If I were to try to continue living in Ann Arbor, I would forever be dealing with all of the people I know would talk about me behind my back and either accuse me of driving Matthew to be gay or feeling sorry for me. I can't stand the thought of either. Plus, I don't want to take the chance of running into Emma ever again. I'm not sure I could even look her in the eye right now. So …," she picked up her coffee, "I'm thinking I'd like to reconnect with my childhood roots and move back to South Haven. I don't have any major baggage here. It's just familiar enough that it feels both foreign and like home at the same time. Somehow, that's exciting to me. Plus, you're here, and that alone is a comfort I had not planned on." She took a big drink of her coffee.

El clapped her hands together. "Now, that's the best news I've heard all year!"

North smiled. "Thank you." She picked up her burrito and took another bite.

"But, I still don't know what you're asking of me."

North rolled her eyes, holding her finger up again while she finished chewing. Once she swallowed, she grabbed her coffee and took a quick gulp. "All that I have here is my one dress and this Chicago Bears cheerleader frock you've loaned me. I need my things. So, I was wondering, if you didn't have anything too pressing, if you would follow me to Ann Arbor? We can load up our cars with my stuff so I never have to go back there again!"

"Oh, is that all?"

"I'll cover your gas and buy you lunch anywhere in Ann Arbor."

"You mean, I'll finally get to eat at Zingerman's?" El asked.

North laughed. "Absolutely. And the best part is, I'll only have to eat at Zingerman's one more time!"

They were on the road within an hour and a half and arrived in Ann Arbor by 11:30. Since it would be well after lunch by the time they were done at the house, North decided to take El straight to Zingerman's. It was tricky winding through the streets of Ann Arbor with El behind her, but she eventually found a parking spot two blocks away from the restaurant. North stopped and pointed at it, signaling to El in her rearview mirror. Now that El was taken care of, she could hunt down a spot for herself. She pulled into a parking space three more blocks away, got out, and hurried to Aunt El's car. El was sitting there, scrolling through her phone while she waited.

North knocked on the window as gently as she could, but El jumped anyway. North mouthed the word "sorry," but El put her hand on her heart and waved her off, laughing. She got out of the car.

"It's not your fault, sweetie. I tend to get a little lost while playing my daily round of Candy Crush."

"That's easy to do," North chuckled.

El put her hand in the crook of North's arm as they walked down the sidewalk toward the restaurant. North glanced up at this woman next to her. El was smiling, her head swiveling in every direction, as she took in the view of the quaint Ann Arbor neighborhood. There was such gentleness to this woman, such deep kindness. El hadn't seen her in close to thirty years, but when she ran into her at the worst part of her life, El … no … *Aunt* El had taken her in and cared for her as if no time had passed. North knew there was nobody in her life, probably nobody in all of Ann Arbor, with that kind of heart and loyalty. If that was what life was like in South Haven, North decided she definitely wanted to be a part of it.

"Oh, my goodness," El said.

They had reached Zingerman's Deli, and as North had warned, there was a line out the door already. She chuckled. "I told you." North looked over at El. The woman was frowning, trying to decide if standing in a line that long was worth it. North tugged on her arm. "Come on. The line moves quickly here."

They took their places in line and in no time, they had moved through the front door and into the deli.

The many choices on the menu boards above the counter overwhelmed El, but once North found out El liked pastrami, the only real choice was Binny's Brooklyn Reuben. North ordered the Cuban and they sat down outside. The temperature was still in the 50s but that didn't seem to bother El at all. Apparently, living with the brisk lake breeze all of her life had acclimated her to cooler temperatures.

"Well, what do you think?" North asked, once they had made themselves comfortable at a table outside.

"It's amazing," El said with as much excitement as if she'd just stepped off an amusement park ride. "I've never seen anything like that. They are so busy, yet run so smoothly."

"Yep. That's Zingerman's Deli. That's one of the reasons why they're so popular—that, and these deliciously sour pickles."

"Well, hello, North," a woman's voice said from over the fence. "Fancy running into you here."

North turned to see Iris Webber, wife of Dr. Jonah Webber, who was the head of the cardiac department at University of Michigan Hospital. He also happened to be Matthew's boss. North wasn't necessarily happy to see her, as she'd always found the Webbers to be slightly pompous. "Hello, Iris."

Iris stopped and glanced over quizzically at El.

"Oh, let me introduce you." North gestured to El. "This is my Aunt El. Aunt El, this is Iris, one of the doctor's wives."

"*Aunt* El?" Iris reached over the fence and shook her hand, obviously curious as to how a Black woman could possibly be North's aunt.

North just let the question hang there. "She's in town today helping me with a project and has always wanted to eat at Zingerman's, so, here we are." She chuckled.

Iris chuckled too to be polite. "Well, I'm glad I ran into you. We're throwing together a last-minute Spring Forward dinner party this Saturday, and I wanted to invite you and Matthew."

North smiled and paused a minute, not knowing how to respond. Then, she said, "That sounds lovely, Iris. We'll definitely be there."

"Oh, that's fantastic," Iris said. "Hors d'oeuvres are at six, and dinner is at around seven."

"Sounds great," North said. "Please have Jonah let Matthew know that I've already responded for the two of us and he'd better be there."

"All right, I'll do that." Iris waved to El. "It was a pleasure to meet you. Enjoy your lunch."

"Thank you," El said. When the woman walked off, El glared at North. "What on earth are you doing?"

North smiled. "Making things . . . uncomfortable."

El chuckled and shook her head. "Child, you best be careful."

Just then, a server dropped their baskets of food in front of them.

El ate her lunch, responding with "Mmmm" after nearly every bite.

North realized this was something else she loved about El. This was a woman who enjoyed good food. North respected anyone who could experience great food with the proper appreciation.

Once they finished their lunch, the pair made their way back to their cars and headed out of downtown.

North began to feel pain in her hands. When she glanced down, she saw, to her horror, that her knuckles were completely white. She stopped at a stoplight and rubbed them together. To say she was worked up about going back home was an understatement. The thought of walking away from everything she and Matthew had built was transforming her delicious lunch into a gurgling mess of gas pains. Should she stay and fight for her marriage? Hadn't she made a vow to do everything to keep them together, for better or for worse? How do you define worse? Just throwing in the towel and walking—no, running—away from it all now felt very wrong.

As she drove, North kept tabs on El in her rearview mirror, eventually pulling into the driveway of North and Matthew's stately Fair Oaks Parkway manor. After hitting the button on the garage door opener, North got out of her car and stood while it opened. Though it was a large two-story with three garages on the side, their house maintained a coziness all nestled into the woods. The trees surrounding their home had sprouted fresh new leaves, and were accented by the bright yellow and red tulips that were popping up each day exactly where North had planted them. The chickadees and woodpeckers were flying around and singing while they took turns enjoying the suet blocks scattered throughout the yard. The whole place seemed idyllic.

El had pulled in right behind her. She stepped out of her car and looked around with wide-eyed wonder. "*This* is your house?" El asked.

North gave her a sad smile and nodded.

"Whew," El said, with a bewildered shake of her head. "Child, you did all right for yourself."

North wiped at a tear.

"Hey there." El walked over and put an arm around her shoulder, speaking softly. "Now that we're here, it's getting real, isn't it?"

North opened her mouth to speak, took a short breath, and closed it. She was afraid she might break down right on the driveway if she let her emotions get the better of her. Instead, she just nodded, her lower lip quivering as she rested her head on Aunt El's shoulder.

"It's all right. You go right ahead and feel those feelings." El wrapped both arms around her. "If this is too hard for you to do today, then don't. You don't have to force yourself to do anything on my account. I'm a grown-ass woman, and I can easily find my way back home."

There was that wit and loving warmth that garnered this woman the title of "Aunt." It felt good to have someone hug her, understand her, and allow her the freedom to unravel her tangled web of feelings at her own pace. She'd never had that from her own mother.

When she'd awoken that morning, North was absolutely sure

that she never wanted to step foot into this house again. Standing here now, though, looking at her home and seeing the life she'd built with her husband, walking away from it all felt wrong. She wanted to stay. She loved it here, and she loved Matthew.

Lifting her head, North looked at her Aunt El, opened her mouth to speak, but once again, no words were coming.

Aunt El smiled. "I know. It's all right."

North did manage an, "I'm so sorry for dragging …"

"Don't be ridiculous, sweetie. I finally got to eat at Zingerman's Deli," El said with a chuckle. "That alone was worth the drive."

North laughed and wiped at her eyes. "Can I at least make you a cup of coffee before you head home so you don't fall asleep on the road?"

"That would be lovely—and I expect a tour of the house while it's brewing."

"Oh, absolutely," North said. "Follow me."

She took El's hand and walked into the garage. To the far left, behind the third garage door , sat a red convertible BMW that caught North's eye. Matt's prized blue model, however, was missing. "What the hell?" North said.

"What's wrong?"

"That car," North pointed.

"It's a nice one," El said.

"It may be, but it's not ours." North walked up the three cement stairs and opened the door into the house. The smell of freshly brewed coffee hit her. When she turned to punch the code into the alarm, she was surprised to find it had never been armed. "Something's going on here."

North walked into the kitchen and saw an Indian-looking

gentleman sitting at the counter, eating toast and jam and drinking coffee while staring down at a tablet. "Who the hell are you?"

The man was so startled, he dropped his toast, before looking up at her with something like terror. "Ahhh … hello Mrs. Cooper." His voice was shaking. "I'm Amit Basu. Doctor Amit Basu."

North finally recognized him. She remembered him from the Webbers' last dinner party, because Matthew had made a point of ignoring him that entire evening. "Oh my God," she said, the horrible realization washing over her. "You're … him, aren't you?"

Amit Basu stood slowly from his seat, shaking. "M-, M-, … Matthew was very upset."

North scoffed. "I was only gone one freakin' night."

"Oh. N- nn- … nothing happened, Mrs. Cooper," Amit said, waving his hands as if trying to clear stink out of the air.

"Get out," North said through clenched teeth.

"I slept in the guest room," Amit said, as if that would make everything okay.

North responded by screaming so loud, she was sure it made the windows rattle. "GET OUUUUUUT!"

For a moment, Amit Basu's whole body shook, as if he were having a seizure. Then, he pulled himself together, grabbed his sport coat off the back of the chair, picked up his tablet, and ran past North and El out the door and into the garage.

North stood there, breathing hard, while she processed this new flood of emotions. She heard the garage door open, then the BMW's engine and the sound of it driving quickly away.

A gentle hand landed on her shoulder. North reached up and clutched it for a moment, feeling strengthened from the love and support that came from it. Then she turned, looked her aunt squarely in the eye, and pointed. "Through there is the master bedroom. There are two pieces of luggage in the closet. Please put them on the bed and open them. I'll be in in just a minute to pack. I'm going downstairs to get some boxes."

"On it," El said, and she scurried off in the direction North pointed.

Instantly, the true picture had become clear. Emma had told her Matthew was inconsolable, but that didn't seem to be the case. Instead, North had spent one night away, and Matthew had been easily consoled by the one person he truly loved—a man who had moved in and made himself comfortable in the home that she'd created. In just one day, she had lost her husband, her best friend, her home, and her entire life.

North picked up the plate with toast still on it. It was part of the set that she and Matthew had picked out together, a chef's white with scalloped edges. Screaming, she threw it against the cupboard. It shattered, leaving a small gouge in the wood. Next, she picked up the cup of coffee and threw that at the row of crystal wine glasses hanging under the cupboard. Her direct hit shattered all but one.

North let out a haggard breath and stepped back to look at the carnage she had created. She didn't want to destroy the place; she had worked too hard on it. Nevertheless, this definitely made a statement, and it did feel good to release some of that rage.

Just then, her purse started playing "The Wind Beneath my Wings." North scoffed and rolled her eyes. She was sure Dr. Basu had called Matthew in a panic to corroborate their stories. She wasn't having any of it. North pulled the phone out of her purse, clicked the call on and calmly said, "Go. To. Hell." Then, she turned the phone off and headed downstairs to get the boxes. She knew that Matthew would hurry home to talk to her, so she was going to make sure she was gone long before he arrived.

Chapter Five

Sunlight was glistening through North's window with beams of light shining in her eyes when she woke up. It felt akin to a personalized divine saying, "North Cooper, get your butt out of bed and get on with the rest of your life!"

She let out a groan, rolled over, and covered her eyes with her blanket.

Just then, as if on cue, the chickadees arrived outside her window and started chirping. She could have sworn she heard one of them say, "Oh, no you don't!"

North pulled the blanket back down, rolled onto her back, looked up at the ceiling fan turning in its silent, methodical pace, and sighed.

The intense anger of yesterday had seemed to super-charge her with the energy she needed to pack up her belongings, at least all the things she could take in two cars, and get out of Ann Arbor.

But this morning, reality was hitting hard, and North found herself overcome with deep sadness and grief that zapped all her strength.

She loved Matthew, not because he was a doctor and provided

her with a good life, but because he was a good man deep down. The thought that he no longer loved her was utterly devastating.

Now, she was all out of tears and found herself lost in a miserable numbness that felt paralyzing.

It was mind-boggling how quickly her present and her future, nurtured and constructed so carefully for years, seemed to evaporate within nanoseconds. Once she'd returned back to the safety and comfort of her room at Aunt El's home, she saw a new text from Emma that said, *"Seriously? You come back, and with no regard for what my brother is going through, you break a bunch of shit and then leave? You are unhinged, North! Good riddance!"*

North had stood shaking in the middle of the room with her mouth hanging open. How could she have been so stupid? Her mother had always told her that blood was thicker than water, though with their tumultuous relationship, North had made it a goal to prove her wrong. She had wanted to demonstrate that friends could be just as loving and loyal as family—perhaps even more so—but this text stung like a glass of ice water being splashed in her face. Shaking off the shock and catching her breath, North made a mental note: do not make the mistake of befriending the next husband's siblings.

Just then, there was a quiet knock at her door. "North, dear," El summoned. "The coffee is hot, and I'm about ready to cook the eggs."

North was stunned. How late had she slept? She was the one who was supposed to be cooking for Aunt El. "I'll be out in a minute," she replied.

It took herculean effort to throw off the covers and sit up, and even more to rise to her feet. It was remarkable how difficult it was to start the day when there was no reason to get out of bed.

She pulled on a pair of black leggings and an oversized University of Michigan sweatshirt before dragging herself out the door to the kitchen. "I'm sorry, Aunt El. It only took me one day to break my promise to take care of you while I was here." She flopped down in a chair at the table and lifted the waiting cup of coffee.

"Nonsense. It's my pleasure to have you here." El walked over and set a plate containing two over-medium eggs, a slice of ham, and buttered toast in front of her. There was also a small ramekin of cut strawberries with bits of kiwi to give it color. "Now, this is not at the level of the incredible breakfast you made for me yesterday, but this is what I can do," El said.

North looked at the plate full of love in front of her. "This is perfect. Thank you." She took a sip of her coffee, then picked up her fork and popped a yolk, letting the creamy yellow ooze run over her ham.

Aunt El sat down across from her and began to cut into her ham. "Do you have any plans for today?"

Plans? The question took North by surprise. She had no plans except to finish her breakfast, then crawl back into bed and return to the dark abyss that was now her life; however, something in the way Aunt El was looking at her told her that wallowing in self-pity would not be acceptable. She would have to make an effort if she didn't want to quickly wear out her welcome. But what was the first step in rebuilding an entire life in a new place? "No. I guess I should get out and look for a job."

"Now that's something," Aunt El said. "Any place in particular you'd like to work?"

North let out a long and heavy sigh; she had no answer. She quickly crammed a bite of ham into her mouth so she didn't have to say she had no clue as to what direction to take her life. She just shrugged her shoulders.

El washed down her bite with coffee. "I could find out if there are any openings at the hospital. I've been retired for a while, but I still know a few people over there who would do me a solid if I asked."

North put a bite of egg in her mouth followed by a bite of her toast. The constant flow of feeding herself became her best strategy to avoid this conversation. North was not in a state of mind to make any decisions in her life. With a mouth full of food, she shrugged once more.

"What is it you like to do?" El pressed. "What did you do in Ann Arbor?"

It was clear Aunt El was on a mission to help, and she realized that not talking now would be interpreted as rude. North had to speak up. She took a sip of her coffee and swallowed. "I volunteered at the Humane Society and did some voice recordings of newspapers and such for the visually impaired at Michigan Radio."

"Radio?" El paused cutting her ham. "You can do radio?"

"I didn't say I could do radio. I mostly read the day's newspaper articles and some blogs for the visually impaired." North stabbed at a piece of ham with her fork. "But I did fill in on-air a few times when the regular DJ was out sick, so, I guess I *did* do radio a bit."

In response, El only said, "Huh," before she let the matter drop. They ate in silence for several minutes until El finally spoke up again. "You probably need to take a few days for yourself to process the events of the last couple of days."

Finally, Aunt El was going to give her a pass.

North finished her breakfast and insisted on cleaning the kitchen and washing the dishes. Once she was done, she walked back into her room and locked the door. Fighting the urge to crawl back into bed and sleep the rest of the day away, she laced up her black Sauconys, pulled on her jacket and went out the door to the backyard. She rounded the house, walked down the driveway, and headed west toward Lake Michigan.

The day was warmer than she'd expected, with light blue skies and small puffs of white clouds floating peacefully overhead. Many people were on their hands and knees in front of their houses, digging in their flower beds and planting the year's crop of colorful petunias, marigolds, and gladiolas.

Winding through the cheerful neighborhood streets, North made her way down to South Beach once more. She needed to see the water—to hear it, to smell it. She needed to lose her thoughts in it, if only for a moment.

She walked across the sand with her shoes on this time, and stepped up to the edge of the water. Lake Michigan was calm today, almost like glass. The water lightly lapped the shore.

North stared out at the horizon. She knew that beyond that horizontal line where deep blue water met light blue sky, was Chicago, a bustling city of millions. Perhaps that was where she would go to start her new life. Nobody knew her there. She could start over completely, get a job at a department store along the Magnificent Mile, and attend classes at one of the many colleges in the city. She could finally finish one of the degrees that she'd begun years before and carve a life out for herself in the Windy City.

She looked down at the waves licking the sandy shore. North felt the loneliness of a castaway standing on the beach of an uncharted island, scanning the horizon for some glimpse of hope. It wasn't far from the truth. But North knew that there would be no lifeboat en route to save her. She would have to be the boatbuilder if she was going to be rescued.

She turned to look back at the town that was to be her launching pad into her new life. She realized she would probably be staying there awhile as she went through the painful process of ending her eight-year marriage. On the bright side, at least this island wasn't deserted. She just needed to find a way to sustain herself, at least for the time being.

North picked up a small flat beach stone, put it in her coat pocket, and headed back up Water Street. As she turned the corner, she noticed a handful of boats were now moored in slips in the marina. As she made her way past, she walked slower in an effort to read the names scrolled on the back of each boat. Walking through marinas, eating ice cream, and reading the clever names that owners chose for their boats was always a favorite pastime for her and Matthew on their weekend excursions. The realization that this small activity they once shared was now over for good created a strong wave of sadness and tears ran freely down North's cheeks. North swiped them away, wiped her nose across her sleeve, and turned her head toward downtown, quickening her pace.

When she reached the corner, she decided to turn left. She passed a restaurant called the Black River Tavern and made a quick mental note that it was a place she would like to try. North and Matthew had made it a routine to search Google for well-reviewed local pubs to try when they were out and about doing weekend errands or on one of their many road trips. First, they would order two beer flights, which they selected together to taste, rate, and share. Once they had tasted all the beers, they would each choose their favorites to divide up, then sip and savor while sharing the house nachos. Sheesh! How many little memories had she built with this man? This one was only beer and nachos, but the nostalgia still surfaced without warning, just like a pothole on a familiar road. North wiped her nose across her sleeve again and decided she needed to ask Aunt El about the possibility of using her laundry room.

Kalamazoo Street followed the direction of the Black River and was stacked with condominiums on both sides. The entire river was lined with mostly empty boat slips, but it was apparent that life was returning to South Haven.

A white Range Rover passed by on her right, and North realized it was El. Her honorary aunt hadn't noticed her—El had no idea what she was wearing or what her plans for the day were. As North stood motionless, she watched El park her car about a quarter of a mile up the road, get out, and scurry into a small brick building, looking like she had a purpose.

North began walking again, but kept glancing up in the direction of the building to see if El would come back out. There was a small sign above the door, but she was too far away to make it out.

While passing a row of condos on the left, North enjoyed the view from the sidewalk and its curve along the river. On the other side of the river, North saw a second marina, this one nearly full of large sailboats. There were some hearty seafarers gathered on the docks, itching to get out on the water. They were probably disappointed that it was so calm. Sailboats need a fair amount of wind in order to move.

Looking back in the direction of her aunt, she could now read the sign. It said, "WSHS Studio, South Haven Shores Radio." North inhaled sharply and stopped in her tracks. She recalled her conversation with El over breakfast, and her mind began to whirl. Was it possible that El was meddling? North was going to find out. She waited for traffic to clear and jogged across the road.

When she reached the building, she was met with a large window facing the street. Inside was a small radio studio with a very petite Asian woman wearing comically large headphones. She was sitting at a console counter, while a microphone hanging on one arm dangled in front of her. North thought she looked bored, with her chin resting on an arm as she scrolled through a computer off to her side.

Before opening the door, North peered through its small, thin window and saw El standing in the next doorway, talking to somebody out of sight.

"No, no, no, no," North thought as she stepped inside. El turned around, her eyes growing wide with recognition and surprise. "Oh, my goodness, speak of the devil. Here she is now."

"Aunt El, what are you doing?" North asked.

El waved her over. "Come over here, sweetie. I want you to meet someone."

North reluctantly trudged through the doorway and looked down to see a short, balding man whose button-down shirt tucked into his jeans made his pudgy belly look like a beachball.

"North Cooper," El said. "I want you to meet Marcus Anthony, general manager of WSHS Radio. Marcus, meet North, the next great voice of South Haven Shores Radio."

"Nichols," North said. "North Nichols." She held out her hand.

Marcus looked at her and frowned. Ignoring her hand, he looked back up at El. "C'moooon. What do you take me for, El?"

"What do you mean?" El said, her voice rising several octaves.

Marcus waved a hand in North's direction. "She just *happens* to stroll on in here the moment you're talking about her?"

El raised three fingers. "With God as my witness, I did not know she would be walking through that door."

"C'mooon," Marcus protested again. "I just told you; this is a small outfit. I don't have room for …"

"Don't worry about it," North said, cutting him off. "El did not know I was coming in. I saw her from across the street, and I came in to see if she was intervening on my behalf. I'm not hitting you up for a job, and I'm certainly not telling her to do it for me." North gave El her best, *stay out of it* look. "Have a nice day, Mr. Anthony." Then she turned toward the door.

"Hold the freaking phone," El said.

North turned back to see her wagging a finger.

"Don't you give me that 'mind your own business' look and then walk out the door. You *are* my business." She turned back to Marcus.

"And you. Don't you go giving me that, 'we can't afford her' crap. This is North Cooper from University of Michigan Radio, a *real* radio station with more than three employees. You can't afford *not* to hire her." She turned to North and pointed at the floor next to her. "Now, you get over here." Then, she turned to Marcus and waved him out of the chair. "You get off your butt, and both of you shake hands to get this party started."

Marcus was about to protest, but El cut him off before he could utter a sound. "Marcus Quentin Anthony, get out of that chair."

The man pursed his lips and, with a cowed snarl, stood up. North walked back and stood where El pointed, facing Marcus, who was at least three inches shorter than her.

He looked up at her. "Familiar with Arrakis?"

"Excuse me?" North didn't know if he was talking about a singer or a new music style.

"That's our system. We use Arrakis Apex to run the studio. What did they use at Michigan?"

North thought back to those days. She never ran the boards; they had specific engineers for that. But she did remember them saying the name of the system once or twice. "Scott Studios," she said. She left out the part about never even seeing a computer screen with it. North was so far into "fake it 'til you make it," mode, she even surprised herself. She had come back into town to build her lifeboat, only to discover that El was already working on the frame. Perhaps she would tap into her adventurous side and play along.

Marcus nodded. "Yeah. Scotts is very similar. You shouldn't have too much of a problem getting a handle on things." He put his hands in his pockets, looked at El, let out a reluctant sigh, then looked back at North. "How about we try this: I'll give you the Sunday shift, ten a.m. to three p.m. We'll see how you do and go from there."

"One day?" El protested.

"El, for crying out loud. What do you want from me?" He held his hands out in front of him, protesting right back. "I'm meeting you halfway. I'm giving her a chance to impress me. I don't know North from East, and I'm certainly not going to give her keys to the corner office because she's your niece." He waved a hand back and forth between them. "Which, given the *slight* difference in complexions, I'm not sure is true, either."

El was smart enough to know when to let things go. She turned to North. "Are you alright with that?"

Given that North not only now had a job in South Haven, but her first real job in at least five years, she couldn't help but smile a little. "That sounds great."

Marcus held out his hand. "I'll see you Sunday then. Be here at six, and I'll give you the once-over of the Apex system."

North shook his hand. "Okay, Mr. Anthony. I'll see you Sunday at six. And thank you."

Waking up on Saturday morning was like waking up to a whole new life. North did not despise the sun or the birds—in fact, she found herself welcoming them. She hopped out of bed and peered out the window to see a pair of robins working diligently on a nest in a nearby maple tree. Depending on how long she decided to stay, North realized she might have the opportunity to witness the birth of the chicks and observe their day-to-day activities. Her wheels began to turn; this could be good Instagram material. North grabbed her phone and quickly Googled the spiritual meaning of a robin. According to worldbirds.com, it symbolized hope and new beginnings. North took a breath and looked back out the window at the birds. A fresh smile began to grow upon her face.

Filled with a new sense of purpose, North headed to the kitchen to make breakfast again—this time, a vegetarian eggs Benedict with baby spinach and a thin slice of tomato, topped with creamy avocado hollandaise sauce and garnished with fresh herbs. She was so full of gratitude for Aunt El, especially after what she had done for her the day before, that she wanted to dedicate her time to demonstrate her appreciation. So, after breakfast, North washed the dishes, thoroughly cleaned the kitchen, and spent the remainder of the morning dusting and vacuuming. Never one to be completely idle, El threw a load of clothes into the wash and caught up on some reading while she drank the lavender tea with a dollop of local honey that North had prepared for her. Once North had finished winding the cord around the back of the vacuum, she placed it in the front closet and collapsed into the overstuffed living room chair. "Give me just a second to rest, then I can make lunch and rake the backyard later."

"Girl, you have done enough today," El said. "My goodness, you're wearing me out just being near you. Use your afternoon in pursuit of something relaxing—take a walk, read a book, paint those rocks you've been collecting from the beach. Find your balance."

At that moment, the doorbell rang. El and North looked at each other, and North sat up to get out of the chair.

"Don't even think about it," El said, closing the book on her bookmark. "You sit back. I'm sure they're here for me anyway." El pulled herself slowly to her feet. "Unless of course, they're selling something."

She walked past North and opened the door. "Can I help you?" North heard El say.

"Uh, hi there," a very familiar man's voice said. "I'm looking for a Mrs. North Cooper."

North's stomach rolled and her body froze.

"Her GPS says she's around this area."

"And who might you be?"

"Matthew Cooper, ma'am. Her husband."

Chapter Six

El crossed her arms, right foot tapping on the floor. "Hmm, I see," she said.

The last thing North wanted to do was get up and deal with Matthew, but Aunt El was now in a difficult position, and North couldn't leave her to fend for herself. She took a deep breath, forced herself up, and walked over to the door.

"Here she is now," said El, never breaking her stare.

When she reached the door, North saw the charming smile Matthew had put on for Aunt El dissolve into an expression of sadness and pain when his eyes caught hers.

There was a long awkward silence as each of them stared at each other through the screen door.

"Hey," Matthew finally said. "I'm glad I found you. Can we talk?"

Aunt El looked over at North, and as soon as she was given a small nod, she unlatched the screen door and pushed it open. "Come on in, Matthew. I'm El." She held out her hand.

“Thank you,” Matthew said. He shook her hand as he stepped through the door. “I apologize for showing up unannounced.”

All of a sudden, there he was, standing in the new world where North had escaped. The source of all her pain had just arrived in South Haven and was now invading her safe space. “Just. Breathe,” she told herself.

“May I ask how you know North?” inquired Matthew, trying his best to form a connection with El after such an awkward introduction.

“I’ve known her since she was in diapers,” El said. She threw a thumb over her shoulder. “She lived in the house next door until she was in fifth grade.”

“Is that so?” Matthew asked, flashing his charismatic grin. “Wait.” He snapped his fingers. “You’re Aunt El? I’ve heard the name.”

El chuckled and began to loosen up. “Why yes. The child spent as much time in my house as she did in her own, and she used to call me Aunt El.”

“Well, it’s a genuine pleasure to finally meet you.”

“You as well,” said El, softening her tone.

“So, North is staying here with you?”

El pointed a thumb over her shoulder. “I have an Airbnb room down the hall. I’ve recently given it to North. But I’ll be honest, the way she cooks breakfast, I may have to add on and have her run this place.”

Matthew smiled. “She *is* an excellent cook.”

“Cut the shit, Matthew,” North broke into the conversation. “What do you want?”

Matthew looked back at her, and his smile instantly dissolved. “I was hoping we could go somewhere to talk.”

“Talk? What is there to talk about? Oh wait! You want to talk about the strange man sitting comfortably in *my* home, drinking *my* coffee and eating *my* food?" North shrugged. "What's there to talk about? Looks to me like your priorities have drastically changed, and I'm *no longer* one of them."

"North," El said in an even tone. "He's made this trip for a reason. You may want to at least hear what he has to say."

North huffed. "Fine. Let's talk."

"Can I, um, take you to lunch?" Matthew stammered.

"Fine. I know right where I want to go." North swiftly walked past him, to his BMW, climbed into the passenger seat, and slammed the door shut. She sat glaring as she watched Matthew turn his head, quickly wave a goodbye to El, and follow her out.

Ten minutes later, they were sitting outside at a wrought-iron table in front of the Black River Tavern. Despite their current circumstances, North was committed to the traditions they had created as a couple and determined this was where they were going to eat. Matthew had tried to navigate a new path by suggesting they eat across the street at Taste, a cute little martini bar that also had tables outside. But North had made it clear: "You want to talk to me, then we go where I want to eat." Matthew had relented.

Their table sat right next to the road where cars zoomed by a few feet away, or stopped at the traffic light right next to them, but North's seat had the perfect view. She could see all the way down Water Street, out onto the pier and the blue waters of Lake Michigan. If the conversation went badly, at least she could center herself with a peaceful view.

A waiter named Donnie, who had two earrings and a sleeve of tattoos down one arm, asked them if they wanted something to drink. Sliding back into their well-established routine, North ordered their food too: one order of the pulled-pork nachos, he'll have the chicken wrap, and a pitcher of the Big Lake Michigan Amber Ale. Matthew, who had always been good at picking his battles, just nodded his approval.

"All right. Give me a few minutes and I'll get those right out to you." Donnie grabbed dirty plates from another table and headed back inside.

Matthew looked around uncomfortably. North was sure he would have preferred to go somewhere quieter to have a more intimate conversation, but she just wasn't in the mood. She sat back and crossed her arms. "Well, you brought me here to talk. So, talk."

Matthew looked directly into her eyes for the first time, and she caught her breath.

Matthew had always said that she knew him better than anyone, and it always surprised him how she could ascertain so much about how he was doing just by looking into his eyes.

In truth, he had the same ability with her, but through her voice. Matthew had always loved the sound of North's voice. It had been his source of comfort, but it was also what he humorously deemed a built-in GPS to understanding her, because he could recognize even the tiniest micro-inflections and immediately know how she was feeling and why. North called it his superpower.

For North, Matthew's eyes had always been his tell. When she looked into them now, for the first time since she'd left, North could finally see his sadness, his confusion, his fear, and—could it be?—pain. He was truly at a loss for words, and North was sure it wasn't an act. Matthew sat politely in his seat across from her, hands clasped together and resting on the table in front of him. His eyes glistened as he held back tears.

North released an audible sigh. At that moment, a small part of her actually felt bad for him and she found herself wrestling with feelings that were beckoning her to lean over, touch his hand, and tell him it's okay. But the reality was that her well of empathy was buried under so much hurt, distrust, and anger that it wasn't going to happen today. The version of North that was sitting here today vehemently reminded her that this poor, sad man across from her was also the man who had betrayed her, cast her aside, and shattered their dreams. This North felt justified in her satisfaction at his discomfort.

Matthew's mouth opened to speak, but it was Donnie's voice she heard first. "Here are your beers."

Donnie set both of their glasses on the table. "Your food will be ready shortly. Is there anything else I can get you?"

They both shook their heads without looking up.

"Okay, enjoy!" Donnie spun around to check on another table. "How is everything here?"

Matthew gave North a weak smile, grabbed his beer, and took a long drink.

North watched him while she sipped her beer. He was definitely not himself. Matthew was a doctor—a cardiac specialist, and a good one at that. He had always been confident, sure, and strong, but now he was none of those things. He seemed unsure, timid, even weak. She wasn't going to help him out, finding strange pleasure watching him twist on the hook.

He stared down at his beer and opened his mouth just as a pair of very loud motorcycles stopped at the stoplight on the corner. He could have spouted the Gettysburg Address at the top of his lungs, and North wouldn't have been able to make out a word.

The two men, both dressed in jeans, white t-shirts, and black leather vests, as if it was some biker uniform, sat revving their Harleys while they waited for the light to change. The entire nearby community of South Haven gave them disapproving looks. The bikers looked at each other and laughed, relishing the disruption they were causing.

Matthew grabbed his beer and took another long drink while he waited.

The light finally turned green, and both motorcycles accelerated down Water Street, leaving a thick and noxious layer of carbon monoxide to drift past everyone eating outside.

Matthew coughed, along with several other patrons on both sides of the street. He took another drink and finally started to speak. "Well, I was going to say that the first …"

"Here's your nachos," Donnie said, dropping the plate down in front of North. "And here's your chicken wrap. Can I get you anything else?"

"No," North said. "I think we're good. Thank you."

Donnie nodded. "Excellent. Enjoy your food." He turned and headed back into the restaurant.

North took her fork and smeared the sour cream on the top of her nachos. Then, she grabbed a chip, scooped up a hunk of pork and a sliced jalapeño, and popped it all into her mouth. The sweet, smoky pork, the heat of the pepper, and the salty crunch of the chip was the perfect bite, and she savored it. She then took a drink of her beer, which cut through the richness of the food perfectly. This was a lunch she was determined to enjoy.

She glanced over at Matthew, who was looking down at his chicken wrap and potato chips as if he'd found them on a city bus. She watched as he picked up his wrap, inspected it, and took a tentative bite. His expression quickly changed, as if he was surprised that he liked it. Now that his mouth was full, she asked, "So, what is it you wanted to say to me?"

He looked up at her, and began chewing fast, taking a gulp of his beer to wash down his mouthful. Then, he took a deliberate breath and spoke softly. "The difficult part is where to begin. I guess the first thing I wanted to say is I'm so sorry. I know you're hurt upset …"

"Upset?" North wasn't as quiet as Matthew, but she couldn't be. Every word he'd just uttered made her angrier. "You think I'm upset? Let me tell you, upset doesn't even come close to how I feel. I'm completely crushed. My heart has been shredded." She was starting to get attention from customers at other tables, as well as people walking by on the sidewalk. Matthew grew uncomfortable, but he stared straight into her eyes, accepting it. "You took our whole life together and detonated a bomb!" North's anguish was getting the best of her, and her voice was beginning to crack. "You wiped out all of our dreams, all of our plans for the future. You *killed* all four of our children!"

Matthew sat up at that last sentence and looked around. "Uhhhhh, we're having a thing here, folks. No children were killed. We don't even *have* children."

"And we never will," North said. "So, if you think I'm just *upset*, think again!"

"I'm very sorry, I didn't mean to sound like I was minimizing your feelings," Matthew said. He picked up his chicken wrap and took another very large bite.

North realized that any more conversation on the subject was over, at least here at the table. She looked at the nachos in front of her and couldn't imagine eating any more. They were delicious, but her stomach had just done a major somersault. She took a drink of her beer, sat back, and looked past Matthew to focus on Lake Michigan's horizon. She let herself get lost in the color blue and found that calmer breaths were now coming easier. She spoke again in a much quieter tone. "Matthew, just looking at you throws me into a rage right now. I say we just finish our beers in peace, but if you still want to talk after this, I know where to go."

"Okay," Matthew said without hesitation. He picked up his beer. "I'm in." He took another drink.

"How is everything here, folks?" Donnie asked, in a bright chipper voice, rubbing his hands together. North noticed that he even had letters tattooed on his fingers, just above the knuckles. On the right hand was S-O-T-H. And on the left was H-A-V-N. It would have been funny to her if she wasn't in such a crap mood.

"Everything's shit here, Donnie," she said, stopping Donnie in his tracks. He looked down at the food, and was about to say something when North cut him off. "It has nothing to do with you or the food, which is excellent."

"Oooookayyy," Donnie said, trying his best to catch on.

"Can you bring us a couple of boxes and the bill?" Matthew asked.

Donnie snapped his tattooed fingers. "Sure thing. Be right back with that."

Fifteen minutes later, they were parked down by South Beach. North had Matthew open the trunk, and she reached in to pull out the large green and gold blanket she stored inside. She had put one in each of their cars for whatever need arose. If they were out somewhere that was beautiful, they had a blanket for an impromptu picnic. If their car broke down, or they got stuck in a winter blizzard, they had an extra blanket to keep warm until help arrived. Today, it was going to allow them to sit on the beach.

They both took off their shoes and socks and left them in the car, before wandering off toward the water. It was a beautiful warm spring day, but the sand was cold on their bare feet. There were many more people on the beach than the last time North had been here, but it still was not the crowd they would encounter during the peak summer season.

North picked out a spot and began to unfurl the blanket. Matthew grabbed two corners of it, pulled it tight, and together they laid it down flat. That simple act brought a tear to North's eye. It was a perfect example of their unspoken teamwork. She wondered if Matthew even noticed what they had just done. Was it affecting him in the same way?

They both walked around to the front of the blanket and sat down, carefully shifting themselves to avoid crumpling the blanket and keep as much sand off it as possible. It was just another example of how they were exactly alike, how they were perfect for each other. Why was Matthew disrupting their life now?

They sat there for several minutes watching the water roll into shore, listening to the low rumble of the waves that seemed to be competing with the piercing shouts of children playing in the sand. In the distance, a giant freighter crawled along the horizon, more than likely coming from the ports in Gary, Indiana.

"I was going to ask you why you chose South Haven," Matthew said, "but sitting here answers that question."

"It's not just this," North said, "though it is a great benefit. This is where my life began. If my life has to start over, I might as well go back to point A."

"And do what, cook breakfast for El?"

North looked over and scowled. "It just so happens that I got a job as a DJ at the radio station yesterday."

Matthew looked back out at the freighter and drew in a long breath. "That's good. Congratulations."

North's eyes narrowed at his condescending attitude. "And yes, I've considered cooking breakfasts for El's guests. In fact, I've even thought about starting my own bed and breakfast here. They do very well, you know."

"I'm sure they do. It's beautiful here," Matthew nodded. "You'd be great at something like that."

North looked over at him, trying to gauge his sincerity. Perhaps she'd misjudged his previous reaction. Perhaps he was just processing and wasn't trying to be condescending at all. "This isn't about me," she said, changing the topic. "You came here to explain."

Matthew looked down at the sand, and grabbed a handful, which he let ooze back to the ground through his fingers. "I don't know how it happened," he finally said. "The connection with Amit, I mean." He pulled his legs up and rested his arms on his knees, looking out to the water. "If I'm being completely honest, there has always been a side of me that I have spent my life trying to bury. With my parents both being church elders, being gay was an abomination—at least in my family. So, I didn't dare explore those feelings any further. I became very successful at pushing them down, keeping them locked away." He paused, turning toward a child who screamed and then laughed. Then, looked back out at the pops of white foam dotting the distance. "The night before you and I met, I had gotten very intoxicated at a party and ended up going home with this guy, I don't even know his name. Anyway, we had this wild, drunken sex. I had never even kissed another man before, so when I woke up the next morning, lying naked next to this person that had somehow released the horrible beast inside me, I completely lost it. I beat him bloody before he even had a chance to wake up, and then I ran—figuratively and literally. I wanted to have sex with the next girl I met to prove to myself that I wasn't gay. I actually met you the very next day at the cookout."

North's jaw dropped open. "So, our entire relationship was just an opportunity for you to prove you weren't something you didn't want to be?"

Matthew looked over at her for the first time since they'd arrived. "No. Absolutely not. Our entire relationship was all about love and respect. If you remember, we didn't have sex that night, which was the one thing I had set out to do. It was my mission. But then I met you, and my mission changed. I couldn't stop thinking about you. We clicked, and our relationship took off naturally."

"Then why this? Why now?" North realized she sounded like she was pleading, which made her angry with herself. She hadn't intended to give him the satisfaction of hearing her sound desperate.

"North, after I met you, that part of me seemed to disappear. I was so enamored by you and with you, that I blamed it on too much tequila. I haven't drunk it since, and I never looked back; but, as the years went by, those feelings began to resurface. When that happened, I would immediately slam them back down and schedule a romantic weekend with you to remind myself who I am. However, when Amit came on board at the hospital and presented himself as openly gay, those feelings came flooding back even stronger. I wish I could call it a midlife crisis, North, I really do. The truth is, I felt lost, and I didn't want to get to the end of my life never really knowing who I was."

Tears welled up in North's eyes, and she fought hard to hold them back. "So, Amit coaxed those feelings out of you, and you realized that our relationship was fake and that you've been living a lie with me all this time."

"That's just it," Matthew said. "It hasn't been a lie. I love you more than I've loved anybody."

"No! Stop! I don't believe you. If our love was real, then no one could have gotten between us."

"It's not like someone got between us. Who I am on the inside, the person I'm truly made to be, is in direct contrast to our marriage."

North began to cry. "You really need to explain this Matthew, because it sounds like a load of shit to me. All I know is that you've decided you now prefer men over me. How do you think that makes me feel? I have gone over it in my mind hundreds of times, trying to figure out what the hell I did that was so horrible, it not only drove you away from me, but from women entirely."

"North, no." Matthew turned to face her and crossed his legs. "This is difficult to understand, even for me, but it has absolutely nothing to do with you or anything you've done. It has everything to do with me denying the realities of my own self. Deep down, I've always known this about me, but I've avoided it by lying to myself all these years. I've lied to you as well. I guess I need to stop the lies. To keep them going would only cause greater pain in the future." He paused and looked out at the water once more. "But I need you to know that I will never stop caring about you. I will always be there for you, North. Anything you need, you'll have it."

"So, we'll just be really good friends?" North asked with as much venom as she could muster. "No thanks." She stood and walked back toward the car.

"North," Matthew called. "Wait."

North didn't wait. She couldn't wait. She had heard more than enough, and now she had to go process this conversation—and the rest of her life.

She reached the car and tried the handle. It was locked. She turned back toward Matthew, exasperatedly throwing both hands in the air. He was running toward her with the sandy blanket crumpled under one arm.

She turned back to the car and frantically rapped on the window with her knuckles. "Unlock the door. I need to get my shoes."

He held up a hand. "Please wait."

"You just said, anything I need, I got it. I need my damn shoes!"

Matthew reached into his pocket, fumbled for the key fob, and clicked the unlock button.

North opened the door, grabbed her shoes, slid her feet in, and bent down to tie them.

"North, you don't have to walk. I can take you back."

"I don't know what you expect." North finished tying her shoes, then stood up and faced Matthew. "Do you really believe we can move forward being best buddies? Well, let me make this clear—that's never going to happen. You've hurt me, Matthew. When you drive home, I want you to think about that. When you call life-wrecker Amit, I want you to feel it running through your veins. I'm hurt, dammit." She started tearing up again. "You've hurt me, Matthew, and now I have to move on, alone. While you … you and Amit can go to hell." She managed to turn and walk away before breaking down completely.

"North, I mean it. I will *always* be there for you," Matthew called after her.

North flipped him her middle finger and kept walking up the sidewalk along Water Street.

A minute later, she saw his BMW slow down out of the corner of her eye as it passed her. When she didn't look up, it sped off.

North stopped, leaned against the railing that lined the Black River, and wept. She was terrified. Her life, which had been so bright and certain only a week ago, now felt like an abyss. Her mind raced as she wondered where her place in the universe would now be. Even worse—how was she going to face her future alone?

Chapter Seven

North spent the next several hours walking the streets of South Haven, doing her best to envision what her life and future might look like without Matthew. Her emotions fluctuated between rage and despair. Perhaps she'd meet a man in South Haven, a real estate agent or a restaurateur, get married, and live in one of the beautiful beach estates right here. Or, maybe she'd be adventurous and make the move to Chicago, possibly meet an attorney or an investment banker and build an entirely new life in the big city on the other side of Lake Michigan's horizon.

Then North would find herself furious at the idea that the thoughts running through her head were the same thoughts she'd had back in high school, except now they contained an extra scoop of biological-clock desperation.

Her dazed wandering took her over the Dyckman Bridge, the drawbridge over the Black River, and before she knew it, she was standing in front of the sign for North Beach. It was a low-set cement structure sitting on the sand, and North remembered her mom and dad giving her ice cream when she was four or five before setting her on that sign for a picture. They had told her it was her beach because it had her name on it. She remembered believing them and wanting all the other people to leave so she could play on her beach alone.

The pier and lighthouse were easily visible on the other side of the river, literally just yards away by swimming, but to walk that far was miles. At that moment, she realized she had become so overcome by her thoughts, that she had strayed much farther than she had expected. North turned around and trudged back up Grand Boulevard, winding her way through the quiet streets lined with a variety of bed and breakfast houses, large and small. The north side of the river was sleepier, more peaceful without all the attractions and congestion of the downtown area on the south side of the river.

The trees were now bright with blossoms of pink, white, and her mother's favorite, the rich purple lilacs, whose perfumed scent was carried easily along on the gentle breeze. It was something she could never resist. North slowed her pace and took in a deep sniff of each lilac bush she passed.

She had always loved the colors and scents of the blossoms, but they made her sad as well. Tomorrow, her first day on the radio, was Mother's Day, and though her own mom was less than a mother should be to a daughter, she was still sad that such an important woman in her life had died when she was so young. It was that very event that had triggered North's father to pack them up and leave South Haven.

Despite that traumatic event, North had a fairly good relationship with her father; although, she now realized she hadn't talked to him in a couple of weeks. He had no idea how her life had just imploded, but she was sure "Mr. Fix-It" would do whatever he could to make things right. On second thought, it was probably good she didn't call him. He meant well, but his genuine attempts to help could come off as interloping, often causing her to end up angry with him and say things she didn't really mean.

At this moment, North decided she didn't need any more drama in her life. She would wait until she had her shit together before letting her father know anything.

By the time she'd crossed the bridge and arrived back downtown, her stomach felt so hollow, it hurt. Why had she left the pulled-pork nachos in Matthew's car? Perhaps that was why he had slowed down when he passed her; he had probably planned on giving them to her. If only she hadn't been so stubborn. Being a true foodie, she hated when she waited too long between meals, and her biggest craving was convenience. She stopped at a hot dog stand called Chomp's, which was basically a large window on the side of a building, and ordered herself a Detroit Coney. Hot dogs weren't necessarily her go-to food, but to North, nothing was better than a Detroit-style coney dog with onions and mustard. She used all four napkins, delighting in every bite.

By the time she'd reached El's house, the shadows were getting long and she was exhausted. North entered her room from the door at the back, took a quick shower, and crawled into bed. Perhaps things would look better in the morning.

There was a quiet knock on the door. "Come in, Aunt El."

El opened the door and peered her head in. "I just wanted to check on you and make sure you were all right."

"I'm safe, if that's what you mean," North said, "but I'm far from alright."

"Yes. Safe is what's important now." El stepped into the room. "Alright will come later."

North rolled her eyes and sighed.

El walked over and sat on the edge of the bed. "I was just worried because it's been hours since Matthew came by and paid for your room, and …"

"Wait," North said. "What?" She sat up in her bed. "He paid for my room?"

"Well … yes." El looked confused. "He said you knew about it."

North shook her head. "No. He just said he was going to be there for me, and then he drove off."

"He just drove off and left you somewhere?" El's brows furled, and she straightened up, angry that someone would treat her North that way.

"Well, no. I walked away from him. He didn't have a choice."

"I see." El's tension relaxed.

"But he didn't tell me he was going to pay for the room."

"Well, he gave me a check for the whole summer, so you can stay here as long as you want." She patted North on the leg. "Now you get some sleep. You have a big day tomorrow."

North watched El walk out and quietly close the door. Then she rolled back over, her head buzzing, wondering what was really going on with her marriage. Matthew's last words to her were, "I'll always be there for you." He had also said that he loved her more than he ever loved anybody. Was it possible he was proving his love to her by making sure she was taken care of, or was he simply mitigating his guilt by providing a temporary roof over her head?

North decided it was the latter, and eventually managed to fade off into an uneasy sleep.

The next morning, North awoke to sunlight streaming through the crack between her curtains. It felt promising as she stretched and yawned, until she realized that it was the day she was going to make her debut on the radio. At that moment, she caught her breath and all promise quickly evaporated, leaving nothing behind but nerves and nausea. What had she been thinking? What made her believe it was a good idea to take a job at a radio station? Why did Aunt El have to be so meddlesome?

North sat up in bed and threw up in her mouth a little. She swallowed and coughed. "Get a grip girl," she said out loud to herself. "Just breathe." She closed her eyes and took a few cleansing breaths, then held her head in her hands. This new life was scary but she had to move forward. She had to push herself, and today she wasn't just *stepping* out of her comfort zone, she was leaping.

She dragged herself out of bed and took a quick shower, not spending too much time on make-up. This was the benefit of working in radio. After arranging her hair into a ponytail, she pulled on a pair of black leggings and threw on a white camisole, a denim jacket, and stepped into her Birkenstock slip-ons.

Next, she headed into the kitchen, where she scanned the refrigerator and the pantry to see what she could make Aunt El for breakfast. Finding a small supply of sweet potatoes, North grabbed the largest one, along with an onion, a clove of garlic, and a red pepper, and got to work assembling a sweet potato hash.

North put the coffee on, and when El awoke, sat her down at the table with a fresh cup of coffee, a plate of fresh hash with two over-medium eggs, and two links of sausage.

"My goodness," El said. "You are going to get me used to some really bad habits."

"It's not a bad habit to let somebody take care of you for a change." North leaned down and kissed her on the cheek. "I'm going to head out."

"You're not going to eat?"

North shook her head. "Aunt El, I'm so nervous there's no way it would even stay down. I'm going to go for a walk, get some fresh air, and try to calm my nerves."

When she turned, El reached for her hand and pulled her back around. The woman looked up at her with serious but proud eyes. "North Nichols-Cooper, you are capable of doing this and so much more. Remember that even when you get so nervous, you think you're going to keel over and die. There is no ceiling to what you're capable of. Do you hear me, girl?"

Surprised by El's sudden seriousness, North took a moment to process what she had said. She smiled at El's firm belief in her, and it gave her a sense of calm. It was strength she could feed off. "Thank you, Aunt El."

El nodded. "You go break a leg today, girl."

"I will."

"Just don't do it tripping on the sidewalk on your way to the station." El cackled at her own joke.

North walked back into her room for her purse, her phone, and a set of earbuds, before heading out the back door. She used her phone to search for coffee shops open on Sundays, and found that the closest one, called Café Julia, was just this side of downtown. Satisfied with her choice, she put in her earbuds, turned on the WSHS station, and headed down the street.

WSHS was an adult contemporary radio station. From what North heard, their genre consisted of popular light rock tunes. She'd heard Pink's "So What," and The Fray's "How to Save a Life" while walking the four blocks to the coffee shop. The songs were introduced by the morning DJ, Janet Lee, who North assumed was the Asian girl she'd seen in the window when she got the job.

Café Julia was a little two-story house, refurbished with an inviting front porch. There was already an elderly couple seated outside drinking coffee and eating croissant breakfast sandwiches. The man worked on the crossword puzzle in the newspaper while the woman scrolled through something on her tablet.

When North entered, two college-aged girls behind the counter looked up, smiled, and offered a greeting. Pastel orange and green walls gave the place a bright and warm vibe, and North instantly fell in love with it. She ordered an oat milk latte with an extra shot of espresso and headed back out into the fresh air to listen to music and walk off her nerves.

Café Julia was right next to the farmer's market and the small downtown park, where she'd eaten ice cream as a little girl. Sipping her coffee, she sat on a bench and turned on WSHS once more. North looked around, relishing the memories that seemed to be slowly returning to her. As if on cue, the song "Memories" by Maroon 5 began to play, and she smiled. "Thanks for being here, mom," she whispered. Sipping her coffee and people-watching, North felt the calmness she was hoping to find.

Cars slowly rolled past, filling the empty parking spaces along Phoenix Street. North knew that in a week or so, parking would be about as easy to find as a woolly mammoth.

Maroon 5 was interrupted by a phone ring. North looked down to see it was her father calling. She rolled her eyes and let out a sigh. She should have expected this. It was Mother's Day, after all. He always called on Mother's Day to console her, as if she was still a little girl. "Hi, Dad."

"Good morning, kiddo. How are you doing?" he said it so kindly, as if she'd woke up troubled about the day—which she had, but not about what he was thinking.

North wasn't sure what to tell him. "I'm okay, Dad. How are you?"

"Oh, you know … days like this just get you thinking."

"Yes, they definitely do," North said.

"Do you have any special plans for today?" he asked, as if she needed something special to take her mind off what was missing in her life.

"Well … actually …" North decided to go ahead and tell her dad. Yes, she was nervous, but she was about to go on the air on the radio. That was something that you should share with your dad. "I'm just about to start my new job as a DJ."

"A DJ? Wow. That's great." To North's delight, he sounded impressed. "What does Matt think about having a celebrity as a wife?"

There it was; the part that she didn't want to talk about, but she'd already opened the door. "Ahhhh, actually, Matt and I have decided to take a little break."

"What!? What does that mean?" His voice changed, no longer quiet and subdued. Now he wanted to know details, figure things out, make plans.

"I'm not sure what it means yet, Dad. That will take time. Right now, I'm in South Haven staying with Aunt El and …"

"Who?"

"Eljerita, our next-door neighbor on Willow Street."

"Oh, yeah. El." North could tell he barely remembered her. "But what happened with you and Matt? Why are you separated?"

"I'd rather not get into that right now, Dad. Not until I have more things figured out." She didn't need him calling Matthew and trying to fix things. She just needed to concentrate on today.

"Did he do something? Do I have to call him and have a talk? What can I do?" Crap. She realized she shouldn't have said anything, not even about the job. Now, her dad was in prime troubleshooting mode and ready to do whatever it took to fix her relationship, like it was a broken toilet handle or a leaky hose. Once he fixed it, everything would be "better than new!"

“Dad. Listen to me,” she said, trying to calm him down. “There is nothing you can do. I am going to be fine. Do you hear me? Everything is okay. I want you to be excited for me and my new opportunity on the radio here in South Haven. Okay?”

There was no sound on the other end.

“Dad?”

“Okay,” he finally said, sounding unwillingly persuaded.

“Okay, I’m going to go now, Dad. I have to head to the station.”

“When you get out of work, you may want to stop by your mother’s grave. She’s buried in Lake View Cemetery there.”

“Thanks for letting me know, Dad,” she said, even though she had no intention of doing that. “I gotta go.”

“Okay. I love you, kiddo.” He was now sounding sadder than he did when she had answered the phone.

“I love you too, Dad. Bye.” She tapped off the call, and the radio began playing again. It was Ed Sheeran crooning “Perfect.” “Ugh,” North said and turned it off.

She sighed and took another drink of her now-cold latte. She had told her dad that she was fine and that everything was going to be okay, like she had complete control of her life. The reality was that she had no college degree, only a part-time job, and she was mooching off an old family friend. Sure, she had everything under control. Not.

All of a sudden, she wasn’t as excited about the new opportunity. She stood up and slipped her phone back in her purse. “Okay. Let’s get this over with.” She trudged off toward the station.

Chapter Eight

It was five minutes to nine when North took yet another deep breath and opened the door to the little brick building that housed the studio and offices of WSHS.

Marcus, wearing stained jeans and a threadbare Yellow Submarine t-shirt, walked out of his office holding a manila folder and a bottle of water. "Early. I like it." He nodded toward the small studio and walked in. "C'mon. Let's get you started. Maybe I can get out of here early, too."

He wasn't the warmest person, all business, but North obliged. She wanted to be alone, too, and spending a day being alone while listening to music seemed like a pretty good way to make a few bucks. She followed him into the studio, and he handed her the bottle of water. "There's more in the little fridge in my office if you need it."

"Thank you," she said, taking it from him and setting the bottle and her latte down on the counter.

The studio was a small space, ten feet by ten feet, if that. It had a large counter that faced the window with three white metal arms jutting up from the center like crab legs, each holding a microphone that hung downward. Each microphone was positioned near one of three chairs around the counter, and a set of large Sony headphones sat just below each microphone. In front of the center chair were two monitors, a keyboard, and a mouse.

The room itself was sparse—just the counter, three bistro-style chairs, and the lonely little bookshelf filled with a variety of CDs. The walls were a creamy beige and looked a little dingy, but fortunately, most of the real estate was covered up by vintage posters of past and present rock stars like The Bangles, Taylor Swift, Train, and KISS. There was a large rectangular white board with "WSHS-South Haven Summer giveaways" written across the top. Below it was a list of numbers through 30, but with nothing written next to them. Speakers in all four corners of the room were playing the music on the station. "Yesterday" by The Beatles was just ending and Janet Lee's voice could be heard making an announcement about the last South Haven High School Rams baseball game of the season.

"Is Janet broadcasting from another location?" North asked.

"Nah. She came in early and voice-tracked this morning because somethin' came up," Marcus said. "I don't allow it on a regular basis. My philosophy is that live radio should have a live DJ for call-in's emergencies and such, but I'm trying to be more flexible and get on board with the whole "work-life balance" thing, ya know? Play your cards right, and you might occasionally get that opportunity, too." He pulled out the center chair. "Okay, have a seat and let's get you acquainted with ol' Arrakis here."

Nervous that she might be in over her head, North took a seat and looked at the monitors. On the left screen, there were lists and blocks of blue and purple. It looked childish and confusing at the same time. On the right was a video version of a mixing console, which looked fairly straightforward.

"These are both touch-screen monitors," Marcus said. "This center list here is the live list. It shows what's on the air, what ran, and what's coming up. These blocks here," he pointed to a section of blue and purple blocks on the screen, "are all of our ads and inserts. You can scroll through them and drag them down to the list like so." He selected a WSHS Summer Giveaway promo and dragged it to the center list, placing it just below the currently playing "Landslide" by Fleetwood Mac. "There. Now that will play next."

The system seemed very intuitive to North, and to her own surprise, she found herself picking it up very quickly. She learned how to search for songs that callers might request and how to record a caller's voice on the air, followed by the song they requested. In about twenty minutes, North felt confident that she could do just about anything asked of her—aside from voice-tracking, which Marcus specifically withheld.

"Do you go by Cooper or Nichols?" Marcus asked. " I heard both names at your … *interview.*" He said the last word with a sarcastic chuckle.

"I'm going by Nichols on the air. It's my maiden name."

"Then your on-air name is Kristy," Marcus said. "Kristy Nichols."

"What?" North said. "But I like my name. Why would I change it?"

"Because you want to sound like someone they already know," Marcus said. "There was an actress named Kristy McNichol, so "Kristy Nichols" will sound familiar to them and they'll want to tune in."

North remembered hearing the name Kristy McNichol, though she'd never seen anything the woman had been in. "Does that mean Janet Lee isn't the other DJ's real name?"

"Nah, it's Ling Lee, or something like that. Janet *Leigh* was an old actress, as well, so she's already familiar to people when she goes on the air, even if they've never seen a Janet Leigh movie." Marcus gave her a cheesy smile, like he was some genius for coming up with his own familiarity scheme. "You think my name is Marcus Anthony? That my parents just named me after a Roman emperor?" He shook his head. "No. I'm Tony Markum from Chicago. Pleased to make your acquaintance. You're Kristy Nichols, of WSHS, South Haven Shores Radio, where we play upbeat music from friendly, familiar people. Got it?"

North nodded. She didn't have the heart to tell him that the name he picked was not that of a Roman emperor, but rather an unsuccessful usurper who killed himself after losing his last battle.

"Okay then. Got any other questions before I vamoose?"

"No," North said, shaking her head. "I think I'm good. I just take over at ten, then?"

"Yep, right at ten o'clock is when you make your first announcement and begin playing our feel-good tunes. Then at three, just take your headphones off and walk out. During the week I've got the afternoon drive shift, but since it's Sunday, I voice-tracked it so I can take a little vay-cay."

"Understood," North said. "Thank you for the opportunity and the training."

"No problem. Break a leg." Marcus went into his office and came back out sliding his arm into the sleeve of a blue windbreaker. "The wife and I are headed up to Saugatuck to help her parents paint a room in their house, so I won't be able to run in here if you have any issues."

"I'm good." North recalled El mentioning they had dated at one point. "You're married?"

He nodded. "Yep. Almost a year now. Third wife."

"Okay, then. Enjoy your painting."

He rolled his eyes and grunted something. "I'm locking the door on my way outta here. Nobody will be able to come in unless you let them in."

"Thanks," North said with a wave. She heard the lock click on the outer door and watched Marcus give her a thumb's up as he walked by the window.

She picked up her set of headphones and put them on while watching the last few seconds of "Landslide" tick away. She listened to the song fade, then the list clicked up and the highlighted line rested over the Summer Giveaway promo, which played without a hitch. The next song was "Can't Stop the Feeling!" by Justin Timberlake. North spent another few minutes finding local weather forecasting apps online to prepare herself for her first weather update, then opened the folder and filled out all of the new employee paperwork. She wanted to have it all completed before her shift started.

After she signed and dated the last form, she straightened the papers, closed the folder, and left it on Marcus's desk. Then she went back into the studio, put the headphones back on, and waited the agonizingly slow last five minutes until ten, her stomach growing increasingly queasy as each minute passed. The last song, "Slide" by the Goo Goo Dolls, wound down, and North's intro was next. She pulled her mic close and turned it on by tapping the right touch screen. "Hi, there South Havennnn … ites. That was the Goo Goo Dolls, and my name is Nor … uhhh, Kristy. Kristy Nichols. I'll be with you on this beautiful Sunday. Now, let's listen to "Material Girl" by Madonna." She hit the 'play' button on the center list and turned her mic off. Then, remembering something else, she clicked it back on and spoke into the mic. "And happy Mother's Day to all of you *mothers* out there!" Then she clicked the mic off again, scoffed, and dropped her head into her crossed arms on the counter. "Gaaah! You stupid … stupid … stupid …" she said to herself.

North grabbed her water and took a big drink, wishing it was vodka. She rested her head in her hand while she went through the binder of public service announcements, or PSAs, available to her. She wanted to find the longest ones and have them ready to go, so she could talk as little as possible.

Next, she flipped through the preselected song titles within the Arrakis system, and she began to notice a theme—all of the songs were very upbeat, toe-tapping, and happy. In fact, "Happy" by Pharrell Williams was the next song in the queue. Though she had only met him briefly, this seemed like Marcus's work. He wanted only songs that made you feel good, played by someone you were familiar and comfortable with. It was like the radio version of Instagram, all bright and shiny. North wondered if there was a rule to avoid reading the weather forecast if a chance of rain was predicted.

For over half an hour, she sat and listened to one overly cheerful tune after another, each song making her feel worse. Listening to someone singing about how great their life was when your life was in a tailspin was like watching *Say Yes to the Dress* after your fiancé left you standing at the altar. North's mood definitely did not fit the current playlist, so she decided to make some changes. "Tightrope" by Janelle Monáe was almost over, and she was ready to trade her first paycheck to avoid hearing Katrina and the Waves belting out "Walking on Sunshine." North was now on a mission. She slid the keyboard closer and typed another song into the search field. Finding exactly what she was looking for, she deleted "Walking on Sunshine" and loaded the new song in its place. Then she pulled the microphone close, and when Janelle was fading away, she tapped her mic live once more. "Hello again, this is Kristy Nichols," she said, pulling up the weather report on the left screen. "Today's forecast for South Haven will be partly cloudy with a high of 72 degrees. It's going to be a perfect day to be melancholy—and to help us with that, here is one from the golden age of melancholy." She clicked off her mic, took off her headphones, and turned up Patsy Cline on the studio speakers. North sat back and sang "Crazy" with Patsy at the top of her lungs. It was the perfect song for her mood … and her life, for that matter.

When her song was finished, the system transitioned seamlessly over to "Just the Way You Are" by Bruno Mars.

"No, no, no," North said. She pulled the keyboard back and began frantically searching for other North Nichols-Cooper-appropriate songs. She managed to find several and began populating a whole new list for a whole new era of WSHS radio: "Someone Like You" by Adele, "Fix You" by Coldplay, "Jar of Hearts" by Christina Perri, and "Somebody That I Used to Know" by Gotye.

With her new list armed and ready, North pulled the mic to her and tapped it on. "I'm Kristy Nichols, here to keep you company on a Sunday. We're going to take a sharp left turn, so hang on, people! I know it's Mother's Day and all, and I'm excited for all of you who are enjoying time together with your families; but in the spirit of being inclusive, there is another group out there that is getting completely ignored. There are people that don't have kids, that *can't* have kids, and many that don't even have relationships. Or, if you're like me, people that just watched their dreams unexpectedly crash, burn, and disintegrate. You are the ones I'm dedicating my next song to. I'm thinking of all of you right now." She tapped off her mic and hit play on Adele. She had just removed her headphones to listen to the song, when a light on her computer screen lit up, indicating an incoming phone call. She put her headphones back on and tapped on the button on the screen to answer the call. "Hello?"

"Uhhh, is this WSHS?" a woman's voice said.

"Oh, umm, I mean, thank you for calling WSHS."

"I've never heard you before," the woman said.

"Sorry. It's my first day."

"I see. Why are you so sad?"

"Ummm ..." North was shocked that a stranger would be so

forward, but realized that she was the one who put it out there. "My husband recently had an affair."

"Gosh, I'm so sorry," the woman said. "That's what I assumed when I heard what you said. That happened to me as well."

"Really? Wow, I'm sorry," North said. "That totally sucks."

"That's putting it lightly. Twenty-seven years of marriage and one day, he's just gone."

The call button on the screen lit up once more.

"I'm so sorry, ma'am, but I've got another call coming in."

"Okay. Thank you for the song," the woman said. "Bye."

"You're welcome. Bye." North answered the next call. "Hello, WSHS radio."

"Why you so down, girl?" A man's voice said.

"I said it on the air. My life just crumbled."

"How about I take you to dinner after your shift, and you can tell me alllllll about it?"

"Ha!" North feigned a laughed. "No, thanks. It's still too soon."

"Okay, well keep up the good work."

"Thanks. I'll do my best."

Before she could hang up the second call, the phone was already ringing again. By the end of Adele's song, she had spoken to seven people, most reeling from relationship issues, and had even received one marriage proposal. Interestingly, each caller had asked about her. It actually felt good to have people out there who were willing to listen, even if they were strangers. Before the next song started, she tapped the microphone again. "Wow, I seemed to have touched a nerve with that song. I just chatted with several people who are in the very same boat as me, so let's have a little fun and take a poll. If your dirtbag spouse stepped out on you, give me a call and tell me about it. In the meantime, here's Air Supply to set the tone." The call light immediately lit up. North started "All Out of Love," answered the call, and hit the record button. "WSHS, can I put your voice on the air?"

"Uhhh, sure?" said a man.

"Tell me your heartache," North said.

"My wife just left me for my brother."

"Oh, that's *horrible*," North said. "I'm so sorry." The light lit up again. "Good luck sir, and thank you for sharing—I'm going to take another caller." She clicked off one call and answered the next. Strangely enough, it was a woman whose husband had left her for her sister.

For the next three-and-a-half minutes, North compiled statements of loss and heartache from several listeners and was surprised by the amount. South Haven wasn't a very big town, but it seemed to have more than its share of people experiencing emotional pain.

During the next break, she played many of the comments back, followed by Maroon Five's "This Love," peppering the instrumental sections of the song with more statements: "My wife left me for a charter fishing captain," "My boyfriend just left me at a rest area and drove off," "My girlfriend said yes when I proposed, and then immediately grabbed her phone to cancel all future booty calls with another guy."

When the song was over, North turned her mic on again and went live. "Welcome back! This is Kristy Nichols, and I'm so grateful for all of you who were brave enough to share your stories with me today. I know a lot of us are dealing with …" Then it hit her. She had just thanked her listeners for being real after she hadn't been real with them. "You know what? I'm going to be real with you, too. My name isn't Kristy Nichols. That was the name I was given in order to be relatable on the air, but honestly, I like my own name better, so let me introduce myself again. My name is North—North Nichols of South Haven, and I'm very pleased to be here with you today. There are many of us dealing with a lot of crappy stuff, but we're not alone. We're doing it together, and now John Mayer is going to join us." She hit the play button for "Dreaming with a Broken Heart" and answered yet another call. "WSHS, this is North, what's your story?"

"No," said a woman's voice. "What's *your* story?"

"I've already told you my story," North said.

"You said your husband left you, but everyone else shared who their husbands or wives left them for. You didn't. So, what's *your* story? How do we know you're not making all this up just to boost your social media presence?"

North felt her stomach clench. She was getting lost in the angst of other people. It was a cathartic exercise; relishing in their pain was somehow minimizing hers, but if she were to talk about it live, it might bring all of those feelings back to the surface. "First let me assure you that I don't even have a social media presence," she said. "Feel free to fact-check that one for yourself. As far as my failed marriage, well, it's still very raw and hard for me to discuss."

"You just praised us for being real and supposedly revealed your real name, but we're still being inundated with a whole set of sad tunes and no reason why. Don't you think we deserve more?" The woman's voice was decidedly agitated.

"Okay, okay, that's fair," North said. "I'll give it my best shot."

"Good," the woman said. "You got this."

"Thanks," North said, as she tapped the call off. Though one of the call lights was blinking like crazy, North didn't answer it. Instead, she spent the time preparing herself emotionally to talk to all of her ... new ... friends.

Once the John Mayer song had ended, she boldly played the entire recording of the last phone call, including her voice. When the recording ended, she leaned into the mic and spoke. "My husband is a doctor in another city where I was living up until five days ago. He had been working a lot at that time, so we made a date to meet at one of my favorite Italian restaurants for what I thought was going to be a romantic lunch. It was a cozy little place where we could be out, but off by ourselves. The last time we had made plans in the middle of the day, he had rented a room at a luxury hotel, where we spent the rest of the afternoon enjoying what we playfully called a "naked day," complete with room service and champagne. That was not the case on Wednesday. When I got there, he looked very stressed and worried. He was shaking so much that I thought he was about to tell me he had cancer or something. Instead, he told me that he'd had an affair." North took in an audible breath and slowly exhaled. "As if that wasn't enough to send my head spinning, he let me know it was not with a nurse. He'd had an affair with a doctor. A *male* doctor." North paused for several seconds as tears welled in her eyes. Realizing she was sitting over dead air, she spoke again, if for nothing else, just to get noise out there. "Ummmm, well ..." She was trying to get a hold of her voice. She knew it sounded like she was going to lose it, and she didn't want that to happen on the air, so she cleared her throat and kept going. "So, my husband basically admitted to me he was gay, after eight years of marriage." She took a deep breath and blew it into the mic. "Naturally, I was upset, so I jumped in my car and drove. Now, here I am, trying my best to pick up the pieces and, like all of you on this Sunday morning, to be brave. So, here's Sara Bareilles to motivate us all through this thing called life." She hit play on the song "Brave" and turned off her mic.

Once again, the phone light flashed. She took a drink of water, collecting herself before answering. It was nice that so many of her listeners wanted to show her support, but she needed to be sure she wasn't crying all over the microphone. She took another long drink and tapped on the call. "WSHS, can I put your voice on the air?"

"You damn well better," said the angry male voice on the other end.

North was surprised at the harshness of the caller's tone. "Can I help you?"

"You ought to be ashamed of yourself, hating on a gay man like that. Do you have any idea how hard it must have been for him to admit to his *own* truth?"

"You're not the first person to say this to me," North said, trying to hold back her anger. "I suppose that if one day decided I preferred someone with breasts and had to tell my husband, then yes, it would probably be extremely difficult. But I need to ask you: why are *his* feelings most important in this situation?"

"They're not, but …"

"Thank you," North said. "And did I mention how long ago I found out about this?"

"Yes, you said five days ago."

"Exactly. Sir, I am not trying to offend you and I'm not coming down on being gay. I've got nothing against anyone within the LGBTQ community. Honestly, I don't. I have gay friends, both male and female, but this is a fresh emotional wound. Can you just give me a little grace to grieve the relationship I thought I was in before doling out judgment cards?"

The male voice on the other end of the line scoffed. "I guess so. I just remember the days when I was trying to come out and how brutal it was. People I had known for years, including some family members, turned their backs on me. Some of them still won't talk to me today, and I can only imagine how it is for this man, an established doctor, to first, admit it to himself, and second, to muster the strength to move forward with it. I'm sure he is terrified."

The word "terrified" struck North. That's the exact term she'd been using to describe her own feelings. To think it could possibly be used to describe Matthew's feelings was an eye-opener. After all, he was the one who put all of this in motion, so how could it be that frightening for him? He was a doctor with a real job.

But then, she realized that things like money and prestige, though nice, hold little value if it means hiding a major part of yourself away just to win the approval of others. "Thank you for sharing," said North. "I really mean that. You may have helped me more than you'll ever know."

"Sure thing, North," the man said. "Good luck to both of you."

North tapped off the call and sat back. Her mind was spinning out of control. Naturally, she wanted to be angry with Matthew. She wasn't ready for the anger to ebb—not even slightly—but the thought that he might be terrified changed things. For as much as he had hurt her, she still loved him, and she wanted him to be alright. The trick was to figure out how she could move forward while maintaining all of the anger, yet reserve a soft spot for him. A juggler she was not. This was going to take some work, some time, and perhaps even a good bottle of wine.

The last piano keys sounded for the song "Brave," and North decided to play the final call on-air from the moment she answered. Once the song ended, she took a risk and answered one of the other blinking lights live. "WSHS, can I put your voice on the air?" She prayed the answer would be yes, because it was too late now.

"Sure." It was another man's voice.

"Hello. What's your story?"

"Same as yours," the man said, sounding very sad and tired. "Two years ago, my wife left me and our two boys to marry another woman."

"That is very similar to my story," North said. "We were just getting ready to try for kids, but we didn't have any yet."

"Yes. It's mind blowing. All I did for the longest time was wallow in a pool of self-pity, wondering how I turned her off from men entirely. But I've since learned that her decision had literally nothing to do with me. She just moved toward the person she was always supposed to be."

"Thank you for sharing that. It helps me a great deal."

At that moment, there was a loud bang on the outside window. North looked up to see Marcus Anthony's scarlet-faced features twisted in knots, looking like he wanted to reach through the glass and strangle her. He rushed to the door and fumbled with his keys.

"Uhhhh," North's voice shook. "I'm going to have to go now." She hit play on the next song, Elton John's "Sorry Seems to Be the Hardest Word," and turned as Marcus's bulky form filled the studio doorway, eyes bulging out of his face.

"This is NOT your public therapy session!" he screamed, pointing toward the door. "Get the hell out of my studio, and don't you *ever* come back again!"

North was trembling. She stood on shaky legs, trying to make her way out the door without falling. She grabbed her purse off the back of the chair, and Marcus plopped down into it.

She stepped out of the studio and heard Marcus cut into the song. "I am so sorry for that, folks. This is Marcus Anthony, here to change the mood and bring back the happiness you expect. Let's start it off with Katrina and the Waves's 'Walking on Sunshine.'"

North forcefully pushed the door open, and let it slam behind her. She ran from the studio for three blocks before stopping to collapse on a curb. She pulled her knees in close, put her arms over them, dropped her head, and cried.

Chapter Nine

North stumbled along, wiping away tears, while making a jagged beeline back home. She crept around to the back of the house, unlocked her door, kicked off her shoes, and crawled into bed, burying her head in the pillow.

There was a soft rap on the door. "North? May I come in?"

North said nothing, and a moment later she heard the door creak open. "Hey, sweet child," Aunt El said in her butter-soft voice. "There's someone here who would like to say hi."

North lifted her head from the pillow and looked up to see El with a younger woman standing next to her, smiling. It took her a moment to realize it was a grown-up Lilly. "Hi," North said. She sat up in bed, wiped her eyes and nose, and tried to straighten her hair.

"My 'sista' from another 'mista!' How are you?" Lilly swooped in with a giant bear hug. "It is so good to see you."

"It's good to see you too," North said, though she remembered getting on Lilly's nerves in the past and would never have expected this type of reception.

"Why don't you come out and meet my grandchildren," El said, taking North's hand.

North took a deep breath. She wasn't in the mood to talk to anyone, least of all kids, but she wasn't going to turn down the woman who had been her shelter and saving grace. She allowed herself to be lifted off the sanctuary of her bed and led into the living room. Lilly smiled from ear to ear and clutched her left arm, like she was afraid North would try to escape.

There were two boys playing in the living room when North entered—one was sitting on the couch, grasping a Nintendo Switch, wide eyes staring into it with great concentration; the other had a handful of small plastic dinosaurs arranged on the coffee table. He was lost in another world, making growling and screaming noises as the tyrannosaurus chased down the plastic people.

"Boys," Grandma El said. "I want you to meet someone very special to your mom and me." She pulled North up close. "This, here, is Miss North Nichols, and she used to live in the house right next door to us when she was your age."

"Hi, Miss North," said the youngest one, silencing the dinosaurs for a moment. The oldest seemed to be in a trance and didn't look up from his Nintendo.

"Eli, give it a rest and say hi. Right now," Lilly said firmly.

Eli stuck his face out from behind his hand-held game and paused, looking puzzled at how this white woman could possibly be of any importance to his family. He finally spoke sheepishly. "Hi."

El chuckled. "That's Eli. He's seven and is in the second grade." She reached down and patted the youngest on the shoulder. "This is Calvin, and he just turned five last month."

"Well, happy belated birthday, Calvin," North said.

He shook his head. "That was a long time ago," he said. Then, he went back to making his dinosaurs growl and scream, while Eli had already returned to his Nintendo screen.

Lilly reached over and squeezed North's other hand. "We have so much to catch up on. Although, Mom did tell me why you're here, and I'm so sorry about that."

Still feeling emotional about the earlier humiliation, North gave her a polite half-smile and nodded.

Lilly tugged North into the kitchen. "Come on in here and sit down with me." She led North to the round kitchen table and pulled out a couple of chairs. El followed behind and sat in the chair on the other side of North.

"We listened to you on the radio," Lilly said. "That was interesting."

"Ohhh, you heard that?" North put her hands over her face. "That was so awful."

"Not really," mother and daughter said in unison. "It was just more talking than what we're used to," Lilly said. "Honestly, I can't believe how you got the listeners to open up like that. That was fascinating."

"Yes, it was, but I thought you were scheduled until three," El said. "Why are you home so early?"

North pulled her hands down. "Because Marcus freaked out and told me to leave."

"What?" El said. "Why would he do that?"

"Oh, Aunt El. He was furious with me. He screamed at me to get out of his studio and never come back."

"What?" El said, eyes ablaze. "He fired you? On your first day? Why that dirty …"

"Aunt El, no," North said, holding her hands up. "Please don't do anything. He doesn't want me there, and radio is obviously not my thing. We can just let it go."

"But you were so good," El said.

"No. I can't go back there." North didn't want to face the rage of Christian Bale's emotional clone ever again. "Please, let's just sit back, relax, and catch up. What I really need is for you both to help me take my mind off of the craziness of today."

As if on cue, El made them all a steaming-hot pot of chamomile tea and emptied half a bag of Pepperidge Farm Milanos on a sunflower plate. The three of them sat sipping tea, munching on cookies, and recounting their lives since they'd last seen each other.

Lilly had gone to Lake Michigan Community College to study nursing and, later, finished her bachelor's degree at Grand Valley. It was there that she met her husband, James, on her first and only blind date. He now taught art history at Kendall College of Art and Design in Grand Rapids, and she'd been at Butterworth Hospital for eight years, which she loved. James hadn't joined them for their visit, as he had opted to drive to Reed City, where he was originally from, and take his widowed mother out to dinner.

North shared the conversation she'd had with her father before the show, and how he'd suggested that she go visit her mother's grave.

"We should do that then," El chimed in.

"Honestly, I'm not really interested. She's been gone a long time, now. It feels like another lifetime ago."

"Well, if not today, at some point we should go. I'll go with you if you want."

North nodded and then changed the subject. "So, what do you guys do for fun?" she asked Lilly.

They spent the next few hours chatting and laughing, one topic easily gliding into the next. It was the most relaxed North had felt in months, but it was abruptly brought to an end when Eli wandered in, leaned on his mother's shoulder, and announced, "Mommy, I'm hungry."

"Oh, my goodness," Lilly said. "We came down here to take Grandma to dinner. We should be doing that. Boys, go to the bathroom and wash your hands."

El got up and went to the bedroom to get ready.

"It was nice to hang out with you both," North said.

El called out, "It's Mother's Day and I want both my girls with me today."

"I don't want to intrude."

"Don't be crazy, 'sista.'" Lilly said. "You're coming with us."

North smiled and nodded. "I'd love to."

After another ten minutes, they were all ready to head out. Lilly grabbed her purse, opened the front door, and there stood Marcus Anthony ready to knock. ""Oh … ahhh … hi. Is North Nichols here?"

Recognizing the familiar voice, El jumped in front of Lilly with both hands on her hips and snapped, "What do you want?"

"Ummm. I want North to came back to the station and work for me."

"No." North stepped beside El and shook her head. "Not happening."

Marcus held up his hands. "I'm sorry I yelled at you like I did, but you should have heard how our listeners reacted after you left. I've never taken so many angry calls with people screaming at me. I don't know what it is you've got, but they latched onto you something fierce."

"They liked her?" El asked.

"Liked her? Get this …" Marcus was smiling now. "They were all saying how refreshing it was to have someone so open and honest on the radio. They were calling her 'True North.' How does that one sound?"

El turned back to North, a look of pure pride on her face. "True North. Isn't that something?"

North just looked down at her feet and shook her head. She just couldn't imagine it. She knew she was a disaster on the air, and she couldn't remove Marcus's angry red face from her memory. This was no longer the direction she wanted to take her life. She held up a hand. "I'm sorry you came all the way over here, but my days on-air are over. Thanks, but no thanks." Walking out the door, she avoided all eye contact with Marcus, got into her car, and slammed the door.

Chapter Ten

Their plan was to enjoy a delicious dinner at Clementine's, an American family-style restaurant in the old bank building on Phoenix Street, but the Mother's Day line trailed out the door, and with Eli so hungry, they decided not to stay. They drove past another eatery called Six Chicks Scratch Kitchen, but it was already closed for the day. At that moment, Calvin and Eli began snickering and chanting the name of their favorite restaurant in the back seat, as if they were at a local baseball game. Captain Lou's, a dockside restaurant serving pub food next to the drawbridge on Dyckman Avenue, was always their first pick, but today was supposed to be El's choice. Lilly looked at El with eyebrows raised, El nodded, and the boys cheered. Amazingly, their timing was perfect, and they were able to get seated quickly at an outside table along the edge of the dock where Calvin and Eli could easily watch the boats passing by on the Black River. They leaned against the railing and waved, giggling when the people on the boats waved back at them.

Lilly and Aunt El focused on their intervention, desperately trying to convince North to go back to the radio station. North, however, stayed stubborn. "It's just not my jam," she kept telling them, though she wasn't being completely honest. Truth was, she had genuinely enjoyed her time on the radio, but as Marcus so bluntly pointed out, it was not her private therapy session. It was a radio station, a place they were supposed to be presenting as cheery and upbeat. Right now, that's not who she was, and she knew she didn't have the capacity to fake it.

"I have an idea—let's change the subject. This is Mother's Day. It's about this wonderful woman who wears three different hats: Mom, Grandma, and honorary Aunt." North raised her glass of Saugatuck Beach Blondee. "Here's to you Aunt El—and to you too, Lilly." "Cheers!" they all said while clinking their glasses, the boys happy to join in with their colas and sip on their straws.

They spent the next hour-and-a-half enjoying their meals, while continuing to chat away. Lilly told the boys it was their "linner," since it was too late for lunch and too early for dinner. "Wait, does that mean we're done eating for the day?" Calvin asked Lilly with wide eyes, his mouth hanging open. Lilly chuckled at her oldest son's concern. "Relax, bud. If you get hungry, you can always have a bowl of cereal before bed." Relief washed over both boys, and they quickly resumed munching on their chicken tenders and playing their waving game.

North closed her eyes, smiled, and pointed her face up to the sun to fully appreciate its warmth. Despite the emotional trauma of being fired earlier in the day, it was the most enjoyable time she had experienced since the previous Tuesday—at least, it was the most normal. It felt good to get outside without brooding and talk, even laugh at times.

When they finally made it back to the house, it was time for Lilly and the boys to head home. Lilly had to work the following day, and the boys had school in the morning—a schedule that required extra time for baths and prepping their backpacks, before even getting into their bedtime routine. Though harried, it was that type of an evening that North had always longed for. Those were the days she had been looking forward to planning with Matthew, but now those days would never happen, at least not with him. Her sadness at the thought was intertwined with fear, as she began to wonder just how far into the future had these plans been pushed for her.

The next morning, North awoke early to make biscuits and gravy for Aunt El, which she completely devoured with delight. She then showered, got dressed in something other than sweats, put on actual make-up, and headed out the door to find herself dutiful employment. Lilly had mentioned that North would probably not have to work once she received the large alimony check from Matthew, but that was not her style. North was someone who had to keep busy. Though she hadn't earned an official paycheck the past few years, she had worked daily, volunteering her time to various nonprofits. She believed in the philosophy that in order to be happy, a person needed three things: someone to love, something to do, and something to look forward to. Since all three had been unexpectedly ripped out of her life, she decided it was time to rebuild. Today was the day she would take back her power and begin the process of picking up the pieces. Today, she would start again at square one by finding something to do.

She started at the Water's Edge Coffee Shop. She was told, in the kindest way possible, that they didn't have any open positions. All their workers are volunteers because the coffee shop is connected with their church. The very sweet lady must have sensed North's disappointment, because she pulled a chocolate chip cookie from the display case and gave it to her for good luck.

North walked down to the park, sat on the bench, and ate her cookie. She was more disappointed than she had expected to be. Rejection was hard, perhaps even more so now. "Stop moping," she said to herself aloud. "She didn't reject *you*; she only takes volunteers. There's a big difference." She spoke the words out loud to practice positive self-talk. She'd read an article that said it was a way to build self-esteem. She took a quick glance in every direction to ensure nobody was in earshot, as she didn't want people to begin thinking of her as the crazy lady in the park. Then, she began to wonder if she was—she *was* in the park, and she *was* talking to herself just like a crazy lady would. Maybe the proverbial crazy lady wasn't, in fact, crazy. Maybe she was … evolved?

North stood back up, threw the wrapper into the trash, took a breath, and headed to the next stop on her list: the Six Chicks Scratch Kitchen. She had no knowledge of what their menu included, but she liked the name and thought that working with six chicks could be fun.

When she arrived at the plain beige building with the red shingled roof, there were already people standing outside. The place was obviously busy and probably needed help. "Excuse me," she said, squeezing past a large gray-haired man wearing a captain's hat, khaki shorts, and a navy windbreaker. The interior was just as plain as the outside, although the metal chicken cutouts attached to the wall created a whimsical feel. The place was loud with activity and had no empty tables in sight. Customers were lined up inside as well, casually chatting away, while silently coveting any table that might be up for grabs. There was a dark-haired man wearing a clip-on badge that said "Mike" at the host podium, looking down at a chart of the dining room. When she walked over to him, he glanced up, pen in hand and said, "Name?"

"North, but I've already eaten," she said, chuckling. "I was just wondering if you were hiring?"

The man named Mike looked at her blankly, then shook his head. "No, we're all set. Thank you." Then he turned to a server who was passing by with an empty tray. "Linda, can you tell Jack I need a table bussed out here, please?"

"Okay. Thank you," North said, and she turned and squeezed past the incoming crowd, feeling completely humiliated. Mike had brushed her off, as if she were a ladybug that had landed on the sleeve of his shirt. In all fairness, she had interrupted him during the breakfast rush. On the other hand, why was Mike there anyway? Wasn't it six chicks who were supposed to be running the place, not "Six Chicks and One Guy?"

The last place on her list was Café Julia. Though she had only been there for moments the previous day, the atmosphere had felt so warm and inviting that it left a lasting impression on her. When she arrived, there were two men in suits sitting outside on the front porch, savoring coffee while studying a tablet and conducting what appeared to be a business meeting. As she stepped inside, she heard the sound of WSHS playing quietly on the speakers. People were parked at tables spaced evenly around the room, drinking warm beverages and staring into their laptops, many of them wearing earbuds. The vibe was calm and relaxed, and North felt instantly at ease. The same two young blonde girls were working behind the bar. "Hi, what can I get for you?" one of them asked her, flashing a bright smile.

"I was wondering if you might be hiring?"

"Oh," she said, looking over at her co-worker.

"I've heard they filled the last opening," the other one said to North. "Are you a barista?"

North shook her head. "No … I, uhhh … just thought it might be nice to work at a coffee shop."

"Oh," the girl chuckled. "It is, actually. But we're all set right now."

"Okay, thank you," North said in her most pleasant pitch, doing her best to keep her dignity intact. She turned around and strolled out the door. When she reached the sidewalk, she dropped her head, let out an audible breath, and wondered what had she been thinking? If she wasn't even qualified to work in a coffee shop, what *was* she qualified for?

North had no other options on her list, because she naively thought she would have scored a job by now. Feeling completely spent and discouraged, she trudged back to Aunt El's, walked into her room through the back, climbed into bed, and turned on the TV. *Real Housewives of Orange County* was on, which made North smile and pull the covers up under her chin in preparation for losing herself in the drama of someone else's life.

Her binge-watching became a three-day marathon. She would get up in the morning, come out of her room to make breakfast for El, then head straight back to bed to watch *Hoarders*, *90 Day Fiancée*, or whatever reality series she could find to make herself feel like there were people worse off than she was. For some strange reason, she found comfort in that.

Aunt El was worried and tried to distract her with invitations to go up to Lilly's for dinner, or head to Saugatuck for a nice lunch and shopping. But North had neither the desire, nor the energy, to leave the house or the comfort of her bed.

Her self-imposed bedroom hibernation was mostly spent watching television, although every now and then, she would pick up her phone and flip through social media. She scrolled through various photos of friends sharing their recent trips, visits with their families, and adventures with their spouses. They were all enjoying the outdoors and being active, especially now that the weather was warmer. The more she perused, the more hurt she became. Her emotions ran on a sliding scale from intense self-pity all the way up to enormous rage. This was a special kind of torture that she had no desire to end. On top of all this, there was the fact that nobody she knew had bothered to contact her or check in to see how she was doing. The circle of friends she used to meet for coffee and lunches or fill the hours of the day with spa appointments had just dropped her. They completely let her go without a goodbye or the slightest condolence. She felt disposable, tossed like a candy wrapper when all the goodness is gone. She felt like an outcast, and she was fairly certain that the rumors didn't paint her as the victim, but rather the harlot that must have created a situation so unthinkable, her husband switched teams. North now realized that she had been coasting through life, living a shallow existence without contributing to anything of real importance; and what made her feel even worse was that this situation revealed that she had no real friends, made no real connections, and was easily expendable.

On Thursday morning, after cooking Aunt El's breakfast, her phone buzzed in the pocket of her robe. Surprisingly, it was a text from Matthew. It seemed ironic that the only person who seemed willing to contact her was the one person who had betrayed her. *"I did it! I'll be by on Saturday. I have a BIG SURPRISE for you!"* it said.

North's heart skipped a beat, and she caught her breath. What did he do? What was the surprise? Had he realized he had made a huge mistake and that he wasn't gay after all? She wondered if he had let Amit Basu know and started playing it all out inside her mind. Perhaps it was a heartbreaking scene, with Amit crushed because he had lost such a good man. North took a deep breath and slowly exhaled; she could almost feel sorry for him. Matthew *was* a good man and losing him, as she knew firsthand, would hurt a great deal. She wondered where he may have driven off to the day Matthew told him.

North looked at the text again, fixating on the words *"BIG SURPRISE"* all in caps. If he was coming back to her, what could the surprise be? Another ring? Perhaps one with an even bigger diamond, to restate his wedding promise and commemorate their newfound devotion to each other? On the other hand, he knew that her love language was quality time, so maybe he had two tickets to Italy and was finally going to take her on her dream vacation to the Amalfi Coast to bask in the sun and drink limoncello!

Her mind was racing with all the possibilities, so she texted back, *"What's the surprise?"*

"HA! See you Saturday!" was all that came back.

North scoffed. Her head was spinning, and she needed to find a way to pass the time for two more days.

"What's got you buzzing?" Aunt El asked her. Was she so transparent that El could tell something was going on just by looking at her? Or perhaps El knew her better than North thought she did.

"Matthew just texted me. He said he did something and that he has a surprise for me on Saturday."

"What could that be?" El asked.

"I don't know?" North said. "Perhaps he realized he made a mistake, and he's coming back to me."

"Did he tell you he loves you?"

North looked back at the text and bit her bottom lip. Those three words were missing. "No. But the words 'big surprise' are all in caps."

El looked back down at her plate of hash and eggs, making a deliberate point to be silent.

"What? You don't think that's it?"

El looked back up at her, concern in her eyes. "I'm not saying it is or it isn't. I just don't want to see you running down a road that isn't there and crash into a brick wall. I've watched you hurting since the moment you arrived, but this week has been the worst. I'm worried about you, and I'm just not convinced this text is a good one." She looked to the ceiling. "But please, Lord, let me be wrong."

North looked back down at the screen; her spinning head now slowed to a crawl. What if Aunt El was right? What if "I did it," meant he filed the divorce papers, and the big surprise was that he was delivering them to her personally on Saturday?

She felt a lump in her throat, swallowed hard, and slipped her cell phone back into her robe pocket, remembering now that she hated surprises—especially when someone let you know they have a surprise for you. All it did was set you on a journey that was sure to end in disappointment, as one conjured up all the 'what if' scenarios. Had any surprise dropped like a carrot on a string ever lived up to the recipient's expectations? In this case of their crumbling relationship, Matthew should be more sensitive to her state of mind. What could possibly be crueler than this? He might have been one of the nation's smartest cardiac specialists, but he could really be stupid sometimes.

North shambled back to her room and crawled into bed. Perhaps she could sleep for the next two days, so the surprise wouldn't be looming over her. She pulled out her phone and looked at the text again. Leaving out those three simple words said it all.

She couldn't sleep, though, she realized, and laying in bed would only prompt her to stare at that text for two days. She wouldn't do that to herself. She pulled herself back out of bed, and for the first time in three days, took off her nightgown and took a shower. She wondered how many times Aunt El had looked at the ceiling and asked for that poor girl to just clean herself.

In the shower, the hot water hit her back and slid down her legs straight into the drain. She relaxed, as the emotions of the past few days slid down the drain with it, and she enjoyed the cathartic experience. After twenty minutes, the water became lukewarm, so she reluctantly ended her bliss by turning off the faucet and stepping back into her cold reality. Once she was fully dried off and wrapped in a cotton robe, she realized how nice it was to be clean again. North turned on her favorite Spotify station and continued her personal hygiene routine. After moisturizing her skin, she blow-dried her hair, then threw on some sweats and began cleaning her room, washing the sheets, and doing her laundry.

On Friday, North spent her time cleaning the rest of the house. Aunt El objected for a brief moment, but soon realized that cleaning was the type of therapy North needed to make it through the day. So, she made the wiser decision to run some errands and stay out of her way.

With the whole house to herself, North turned on some Maroon 5 and began her mission. She dusted, vacuumed, and even washed the windows inside and out, including scrubbing the screens. By the end of the day, she was completely exhausted and ready to fall into a sound sleep the moment her head hit the pillow.

When Saturday arrived, North hopped from her bed, preparing to cook eggs Benedict for Aunt El. Just before she cracked the eggs, she typed out a quick text to Matthew. *"What time can I expect you?"* She thought that sounded utilitarian, without giving away the fact that her insides were doing somersaults.

"11ish," was the response.

She took a deep breath. She could work with that. North knew she could easily keep busy for the next four hours. Her hands worked diligently, making El her signature eggs Benedict, with a supremely smooth, scratch-made hollandaise sauce.

When breakfast was over, and she had listened to El's praise, she cleaned up the kitchen, made her bed, tidied up her room, took a shower, and dressed in curvy denims and a white camisole. Her dishwater blonde hair was clean, shiny, and draped smoothly over her shoulders, and she wore just enough make-up to look fresh but effortless.

The doorbell rang as she was applying a clear coat of gloss to her lips, and she heard El's voice say, "Good morning, Matthew. Come on in."

North walked into the living room to see Matthew dressed in faded jeans, a white button-down shirt and a navy sport coat.

"Hey there," he said, smiling brightly. "Are you ready?"

"I guess so," she said, crossing her arms. "So, what's the big surprise?"

Matthew reached back, opened the door and nodded toward it. "Come with me, and I'll show you."

"Wait, you can't tell me? We have to go somewhere?"

"I have to *show* you."

North took a deep breath and glanced over at El, who stood there with a subtle noncommittal smile on her face. She looked back and jerked her head toward the door. "Okay," she exhaled, as she uncrossed her arms and headed out the door. "I'll see you later, Aunt El."

"All right, then. Have a good time."

"Thank you," Matthew said, following North outside.

Seconds later, they were traveling in his BMW toward town. Matthew repeatedly glanced her way, chuckling with a child-like sense of giddiness. He was definitely excited to show her something.

They were driving up Kalamazoo Street, when North thought she saw the words "True North" written in bold black letters on a piece of paper taped to a light pole. "Stop!" she yelled at Matthew.

He slammed on the brakes and pulled to the side of the road. "What is it?"

North jumped out of the car and ran back to the pole to see what was on the paper. She had read it right. The page had "True North" in bold, followed by smaller text that read, "Come back on the air!"

"What's that?" Matthew asked, walking up.

North shook her head. "It's some stupid stunt by the guy who runs the radio station. I think it's his way to lure me back."

"Well, why don't you …"

"No. I'm not going back there, and we're not talking about it." She sat in the car. "Come on, let's get this surprise thing over with."

Matthew got back into the car and didn't bring it up again, that is, until they passed by the little brick studio building. "Whoa, look at that."

North looked over to see the front of the building plastered with the same signs, along with a big, bright-green poster that said, "True North Come Back!"

North scoffed and shook her head. "He's such a jerk."

"Well, he's going to pretty great lengths to get you back."

"It isn't going to work. He has anger issues and he treated me horribly. I'm not going back into that environment again."

Matthew let it drop. He continued on, crossed over the Dyckman drawbridge and turned down the peaceful streets on the north side of the river, eventually stopping the car on Grand Boulevard. He smiled at her and got out of the car.

"What?" she said. "Are we walking from here?"

He leaned back in. "You could say that."

North rolled her eyes. "Okay," she said. She opened her door and got out. Matthew stood behind the car, arms crossed, Cheshire Cat smile plastered across his face. She walked back to stand next to him. "Okay. Now what?"

Matthew nodded at the house in front of him. "Check it out."

North turned around to see an old Victorian house, weathered, dark-blue paint chipping off everywhere, with a white wraparound porch that had been worn down to the bare wood up the center of the steps. It had an old ornate cupola on top, but the window was so dirty she couldn't see inside. Her eyes followed the stringy, dry bushes in front of the porch, to the clusters of weeds throughout the grass- barren yard, all the way to the real estate sign stuck in the ground that said “Sold.”

“What is this?” She turned back to Matthew, who stood with his left hand in his pocket, smiling gleefully at her.

“This,” he said, pulling his hand out of his pocket and jingling a set of keys in front of her, “is yours.”

Chapter Eleven

"What the hell?" North demanded. She looked up at the house and back at Matthew with her hands flailing in the air. "What do you mean, 'It's mine?'"

"I bought it for you," Matthew said, unable to stop smiling. "Here." He jingled the keys again. "Go take a look at your new house."

North looked back up at the monstrous aged Victorian, and a wave of nausea hit her. Not only had she lost her beautiful home in the idyllic Burns Park neighborhood of Ann Arbor, but she had now been given this aging wreck of a house as what … a consolation prize? She became instantly overwhelmed with the burden of it all. "But … why?" She looked back at Matthew, who still had that dumb-ass smile on his face that she just wanted to punch. "Why would you do this to me?"

His smile faded. His brows furled, and his head cocked to one side, confused, like a little Shih Tzu trying to figure out where its owner had hidden its treat. "Do, *to* you?"

"Yes!" North screamed. "What could I possibly have done to you that was so bad, you felt the need to exile me from my own home?

The home that I meticulously decorated and loved, only to saddle me down on the other side of the state with …" she pointed to the house, "this … thing!"

Matthew frowned and pulled the keys back. "I thought you'd be excited about this."

"Why, Matthew? What would make you think I would possibly want an old, beat-up house?" She reached out with both hands and shoved him back. "This is your way of getting rid of me, isn't it? You just want to lock me up in this piece of shit, so you can move on, guilt-free, with your shiny life and your new doctor-lover. That's what you're doing, isn't it?" She shoved him back again.

"No," Matthew shook his head.

"You bought your wife an entire house. You've taken care of her. Now you have nothing to worry about."

"That's not it, North."

"You no longer have to feel bad about living in the house with your boyfriend—the house that your wife fixed up so beautifully. She's got another project to work on, now."

"There is no boyfriend," Matthew fired back. "Amit's gone."

North stopped, caught her breath. "He's gone?"

Matthew put his hands in his pockets, looked at the ground, and nodded. "He left me."

North took a step back. "Why?"

Matthew nodded his head in the direction of the house. "Because of this."

North looked up at the house again, paint chipping off the old wooden siding. She held up her hands and shook her head. "Wait. Help me understand this. Your boyfriend left you because you bought your wife a piece of shit house?"

"It's not a piece of shit, it's a fixer-upper," Matthew said, an irritated edge to his voice. "I actually got into a bidding war over this house. I paid much more for it than it's worth, but I got it because I was able to pay cash for it. I did that for you."

"You paid …" the word caught in her throat. "Cash?"

Matthew looked up at her and nodded sadly.

"Like … from our savings?"

Matthew nodded again.

North's legs felt wobbly. "Oh. My. God." Her voice cracked, her vision blurred, and she felt as if she might vomit at any moment. Was this what a panic attack felt like? She stumbled over to the curb and dropped down, breathing heavily.

"North?" Matthew stepped over to her and put his hand on her shoulder. "North, honey. Breathe."

North flinched from his touch, as if it were a hot poker burning through her skin. "*Don't* touch me!" A rage bubbled up from inside her, clearing her nausea and her eyesight. She jumped from the curb, stood directly in front of him, and pointed her finger an inch from his nose. "You took everything we had and dumped it into this money pit without even talking to me." Matthew stumbled back, feeling her hot breath on his face, his eyes wide with terrified surprise. "How *dare* you!" She seethed through her clenched teeth.

"North," Matthew pleaded. "I did this for you."

"No! You did this *to* me." She pointed to the house. "You did this to lock me down on the west coast, so that I would be forever out of your hair, and you could go on with your life, faultless and free." She stiffened her back and began mimicking him. "Huh. I bought her a house with cash. I don't know what she's bitchin' about." She shot him another fiery glare. "Is that it?"

Matthew let out a heavy sigh, his shoulders slumped and his head drooped. "I'm sorry, North. I honestly thought I was doing a nice thing for you."

"No. You were doing a nice thing for *you.*" North fired back. "And you haven't been honest with me since the day we met, so don't try that bullshit on me, either."

Somehow Matthew's shoulders slumped a little more, his head drooping low enough now, it could almost touch the ground.

North was over it. She couldn't look at the house, and she didn't have any more words for Matthew. She took a deep breath, walked past him, and headed back down Grand Boulevard, past the other quiet, well-kept homes in the neighborhood. In her peripheral vision, she noticed that people were standing out on their porches and front yards, gazing in her direction. She couldn't blame them, as she was sure their altercation was the loudest thing that they'd heard all year. They were certainly justified to see what all the fuss was about. She should probably have looked up, given a small wave, and apologized for the noise, but right now, she was so angry and embarrassed, she couldn't speak to anyone. She needed to be alone to process this turn of events and contemplate her life without a safety net.

Matthew pulled his car up next to her. "North, get in."

She didn't look at him. "Go away."

"North, you don't have to walk all the way back. I can drive you to El's, and I won't say a word."

North's eyes were laser-focused ahead, and she continued walking at a measured, steady pace.

"Will you at least take the keys?" He held them out the window toward her, but she made no move to accept them. She felt that doing so would acknowledge that his idiotic gesture was okay. "Fine." He pulled his hand back and accelerated away.

North snarled at the back of his car. How dare he act angry at her.

She had every right to punish him, to make him pay and make him suffer for being a lying, cheating bastard. She didn't, yet he continued to make every move to extract her from his life.

Perhaps she needed to change. Perhaps she needed to use her anger constructively and go on the offensive. She was, in fact, the woman who was scorned. She could get a lawyer and fight for her home in Ann Arbor. He could park his cheating ass in the mega-shack he'd just purchased with their entire savings. He could resign from his posh position at University of Michigan Hospital and get a job at the hospital in South Haven.

She crossed the Dyckman Bridge and headed toward downtown, hardly noticing where she was because her thoughts were racing through her head.

The cold, hard truth was that if she forced Matthew to give up everything, the results would only punish her more. With her lack of education, she didn't have the ability to secure a job that would pay enough to support her current lifestyle or the mortgage on their Ann Arbor home. Plus, if Matthew gave up his current position, the alimony he would be ordered to pay her would probably be greatly reduced.

Alimony? That was the first time that word had passed through her mind. Did that mean she was succumbing to her fate as a divorced woman? Matthew hadn't brought up divorce yet. Was that yet another ploy? If she were to bring it up, would the failure of the marriage be placed on her, thereby reducing the amount he would owe her? She didn't think that sounded right, but she wasn't sure how these things worked. The only thing she was sure of was the fact that she no longer trusted Matthew. Whether out of malice or sheer stupidity, his current default was to cause her pain.

Suddenly, she saw her name out of the corner of her eye. Startled, she looked up and realized she was standing right across the street from the little white brick WSHS studio, where a large poster plastered on the window read, "True North, PLEASE Come Back!"

"Seriously?" she whispered under her breath. How dare that temperamental jerk treat her so horribly, then try to bait her back with a dramatic public apology. He may have thought that this town was his stage, but she was no longer one of his performers. He was a nobody, and maybe it was high time somebody let him know that.

North marched across the street toward the studio.

Chapter Twelve

As she approached the building, North could see the young Asian woman sitting in the studio, headphones on, oblivious to anything going on outside the window.

Reaching the side of the building, North grabbed the top of the banner and, with one long swish, ripped it off the wall and crumpled it into the smallest ball she could manage. Then, with satisfaction and confidence, she opened the door to the little station and marched back to Marcus's office. The light was on, but he was not in. She spun to see that the DJ had finally noticed her. The woman had her headphones off and was standing in the doorway. She wore blue floral shorts, a pale green button-down shirt with the long sleeves rolled up to her elbows, and cheap rubber flip-flops. Her dainty hands were gripping the doorjambs, and her dark eyes were wide with fright.

Instantly, North was disarmed. She had no gripe with this woman and certainly did not want to scare her. "Is Marcus coming back?"

"I don't think so," the woman said. "He rarely comes in on Saturdays, unless there's a promotion going on."

North held up the crumpled banner in her hand. "Well, when you see him, can you please tell him to stop putting these stupid signs up? I'm not coming back here."

"He doesn't put them up."The woman relaxed, releasing the door-

jamb, and crossed her arms. "People do."

"People? What people?"

The woman shrugged. "Random people. Marcus takes them down as soon as he sees them, but people keep putting new ones back up."

"You're kidding me."

The woman shook her head. "No. Apparently, you made quite an impression."

North paused for a moment and licked her top lip, trying to process what she'd just heard. She stared at the crumpled paper in her hand, finally lowering it. She didn't know what to make of it now. She had seen the signs posted around town, and because she believed Marcus to be the instigator, it fueled her anger each time she saw them. She didn't know what to do with this new information, and with everything that had just happened with Matthew, she couldn't figure it out here. She would need time to process her jumbled mess of feelings.

"Okay. Thank you," she said, without looking back up at the DJ. She bolted out the door, closing it a bit too hard, and walked at a brisk pace up Kalamazoo, past Phoenix Street, and back toward Aunt El's, cradling the balled-up banner under one arm like a football.

Ten minutes later, she unlocked the back door to her room, climbed upon the bed, and sat cross-legged. She placed the ball in front of her and stared at it, as if it were some ancient talisman that would somehow give her a signal from a higher power to choose the direction for her life.

Was it possible that people—the actual listening audience that particular day—genuinely appreciated her honesty so much that they were willing to create a poster campaign to entice her back? North could not make sense of it. No one had ever fought for her before. Not like this.

There was a quiet knock on the door and El's soft voice from the other side. "North, honey? Can I come in?"

"Sure," North said, still staring at the paper ball.

The door opened and El walked across the room to sit gently on the side of the bed. "What's this?"

"It's a poster that somebody put up at the radio station to get me to come back."

"To get you to come back?" El asked. "Back on the air?"

"Yes."

"Then why is it all crumpled up?" El picked up the ball and began to unravel it.

"Because I thought Marcus did it," North sighed. "I thought he was trying to apply public pressure in order to get me back on the air so he could save face and look like the hero for trying, instead of the jerk with anger management issues that ran me out."

El stood and smoothed out the large poster against the quilt. "True North, please come back." El read. She chuckled. "Isn't that something?"

North let out an exasperated groan and fell back on her pillow. "I don't know what to do about anything anymore. I don't even know how I'm supposed to be feeling right now."

El pushed the poster aside and sat back down on the bed. "I would think, flattered. Flattered that someone cares enough about you to put this much effort into getting you back."

"Matthew doesn't want me back."

"I see." El leaned forward and patted North's shoulder. "This isn't about the community, the station, or even Marcus. It's about Matthew."

North burst into tears. "The one person I love doesn't love me back, and the only ones who will fight for me really don't know me. If they did, they probably wouldn't fight for me, either."

"Oh, I see." El pulled her hand back. "You wanted a pity party, and I interrupted you."

"I don't want a pity party. I want my life back." North wiped at her eyes. "I want my husband back."

"Your husband is incapable of loving you the way you need to be loved, but he is doing what he can to help you move forward without him."

North sat up. "Do you know what he did to me?"

"I know what he did *for* you. He bought you a house near the beach in South Haven, Michigan. Can you comprehend the amount of love he has for you to do such a thing?" El shook her head. "My goodness, it's remarkable."

"How did you know?"

El nodded toward the door. "The keys are sitting on the kitchen table. He dropped them off and let me know his little surprise didn't go over so well."

"And why would it?" North said. "He made a decision about my life without talking to me. Am I supposed to feel grateful that my husband purchased a huge project for me for the sole purpose of distracting me from his new ... love of his life?"

"His love of his life isn't with him anymore," El said. "And do you know why?"

North remembered him mentioning that, but she never let him say anything more about it. She shook her head.

"Because the two of them got into a big fight over Matthew using every last cent he had saved to pay cash for that house. He told him it was completely reckless, ill-advised, and he couldn't support it."

North scoffed. Apparently, she and Amit had more in common than she thought. Could he be the male version of her?

"He also said," El continued, "that his actions clearly exhibited that Matthew still loved you, and that he refused be in a three-way relationship." El reached up and wiped away one of North's tears with her thumb. "You see, honey, Matthew does care about you. His feelings for you have motivated him to walk away from his own happiness in order to ensure you're alright. His plan wasn't to completely immerse you in a project to keep you out of his life. In the scheme of things, he was looking at the bigger picture—your long-term future. What he did was akin to throwing himself on a sword to make sure you were taken care of."

"Hmmm. Maybe …" North dared to think it. "So, he still wants to be my husband?"

El sighed and shook her head. "Oh girl, you can't ask a bird not to fly. He loves you, yes, with all of his heart, just like I love you with all of mine; but he can't be the man you need him to be, and I don't want to see you continue running into the same brick wall, hoping it will crumble. You'll only end up scratched and bruised over and over again."

North's head drooped, and she cried once more. "Then what am I supposed to do?"

Aunt El put her hands around her, patted her back, and smoothed her hair. "There, there, sweet child. I'm here for you."

"But you can't be here for me forever," North said. "What am I supposed to do then? Who's going to be here for me after you?"

Aunt El grasped her by the shoulders, pushed her chin straight up and looked her in the eye. "How about *you*?"

"What?"

"That's what I thought." El reached over, pulled a couple of tissues from the box on the nightstand, and handed them to North. "Dry your eyes. It's time for the tough love to start."

North took the tissues and did as she was told. "What do you mean, tough love?"

"I've sat back and haven't said a word," El said. "You took a hard hit to the chin, and I knew you needed time to get your bearings, but I can't sit back and watch you flounder waiting for the next person to rescue you, when I know you have the strength to do it for yourself."

North crumpled the tissue in her hands. She knew better than to try to say anything right now. Aunt El was fired up.

"Because I don't believe in unsolicited advice, I made the decision to keep my mouth shut and not interfere in your life. But since you just asked me a question, I'm happy to break my silence."

"Wait," North said, putting a hand up. She couldn't let this one go. "You went off and got me a job at the radio station without my request or permission. That's *totally* interfering."

"I was just trying to provide you with a reason to get out of bed, and it's turned out to be good, hasn't it?" She clicked her tongue, grabbed the edge of the poster, and held it up. "You've got all these people clamoring for you to get back on the air. I didn't put all those posters up around town; people in the community did—people who liked what they heard." Aunt El poked North in the shoulder. "And you're either too blind or too stubborn to see that." El was scowling now. She almost looked angry. "You came to South Haven for a reason. I know you said you got into your car and just drove, but something pulled you here, some inner voice. But ever since you arrived, you stopped listening to that voice. It has given you two great opportunities, and all you can do is sit here and lament about what you no longer have. What's worse, is that it is blinding you to the possibilities of what you *can* create." She poked North again. "If all you're going to do is continue to cry over what is lost, then I can't help you. I can point out what I think is wrong, but I can't do anything more." El stood. "The next move is yours. You can tell Marcus to kiss your ass and disappoint all of your newfound fans, and you can sell that house, take the money and move to Chicago, Timbuktu, or wherever, and start fresh. But, mind what I'm saying: the keyword is '*start.*' You can't just move to Chicago, lock yourself in your room, and cry all day, or you won't be any better off there than you are here. You have to move, so the question you have to answer is, are you going to start in Chicago, a cold city where you know absolutely nobody? Or, are you going to start here in South Haven, where you already have a nest of people who care about you?" She reached down and held up the poster again. "And others who just want you to be a small part of their lives." El stood back up. "The choice is yours, North, just like the power is yours. Nobody else's." With that, Aunt El turned, walked out the door, and let it close.

A muffled, "I love you, child," was heard through the door.

Chapter Thirteen

Exactly thirty-eight minutes after Aunt El closed the door to her room, North swallowed hard and turned the doorknob of the little downtown radio station, but this time it was locked. She knocked, but no one came.

North took some time to process Aunt El's words and let them sink in. Listening to them was akin to an auditory bee sting, and she winced thinking about them. No one wants to shoulder the burden of the work, especially when they don't feel they were the one at fault, but North realized she had to get over it. Aunt El's "tough love" had helped bring some clarity to a very cloudy situation. She dried her eyes and splashed her face with cold water, then got into her car and drove back to the station. If she was going to start her life over, North couldn't think of a more beautiful place to do it than South Haven.

She stepped down to the big studio window and peered in. The young woman who called herself Janet Lee was once again sitting at the counter with her headphones on, staring into her phone. She was still completely oblivious to anything happening beyond her little room. The only difference now was that the door was locked, eliminating the potential for angry women to barge in.

North bent over and tapped on the window, but the DJ didn't hear her with the headphones on. She tightened her fist and rapped again with added force, waving her other hand in the air to call more attention to herself.

The DJ jumped, and looked up with eyes wide and bulging.

North mouthed "I'm sorry," and pointed in the direction of the door.

The message got through, as the young woman took off her headphones and headed out of the room.

North walked back to the door just as it opened.

Janet Lee stood in the opened crack of the doorway, not letting North in. "What's up?"

"Uh … I'm North, by the way." She stuck out her hand.

"Yeah." The woman reached out and shook it. "Li."

"Janet?"

"Oh," the woman chuckled. "Sure."

"Janet's not your real name, is it?"

"No. It's Li, but Marcus thought Janet would be more appealing to the American audience."

North nodded. "He wanted me to use Kristy."

Li nodded toward one of the many pieces of paper stuck to the side of the building that said 'True North.' "North seems to have worked out pretty well for you."

North looked at all of the mini-posters randomly taped to the side of the building. Like a shot of adrenaline, they gave her a renewed sense of energy and maybe even purpose.

"I've got a proposition for you," North said.

"What's that?"

"How about I make my return to WSHS now? On your show?"

"What? Seriously?" Li smiled for the first time. "That could be fun! But should we call Marcus first?"

"No way." North held up a hand and shook her head. "I still have PTSD from our last conversation. If I'm really going to do this, I need to find the courage to take a test drive before I have to deal with him again."

Li gave a nod, waved her in, and together, they headed back into the studio. Li sat down in the chair, put her headphones back on, and pulled the mic up close, waiting for "The Reflex" by Duran Duran to finish.

North quietly closed the door, locked it, and followed her into the studio.

Li gestured to the chair to the right of her. "Go ahead and sit there, we can do this right now."

North took her seat, pulled the mic up close, and put on her headphones. "The Reflex" hadn't quite finished when Li faded it out. "I have a big surprise for my WSHS friends," she said. It was funny to North that Li appeared so shy and soft-spoken in person, but her radio personality oozed confidence and was both bright and personable. "Sitting right next to me in the studio is none other than North Nichols, whom many of you refer to as True North. Welcome back, True North!"

It took North a moment to respond. She was caught up in watching Li talk about her, hardly believing it was real. "Oh, uh, hi. Thank you. It's nice to be here."

"So, tell us, why are you here? What made you decide to wander into the studio today?"

"Well, to be honest, it was the signs. I was just so moved by all of the signs of support I saw hanging all over town."

"Yeah, that's been something hasn't it?"

"It truly has," North said. " I decided that if the listeners find value in what I have to offer, I might as well take a chance and give this radio thing another shot."

"That's terrific news!" Li said. "Did you hear that, everyone? True North is coming back to WSHS."

"I am, and if we're going to do the True North thing," North said, "let's start right now with you."

"With me?"

"Yes. For example, Janet isn't your real name, is it?"

Li frowned. She was not happy that she was put on the spot and showed it by narrowing her eyes at North. "Actually, no. It isn't," she said, but the tone in her voice remained bright and did not give away her feelings. "It's my on-air name."

"So why don't you go ahead and tell us what your real name is."

"Well, if I did that, I would no longer need my on-air name."

"Perhaps you don't. We'll see."

Li's face was bright red now, and North thought she could almost see steam coming out of her ears. She leaned close to the mic and said, "Li."

"So, your name is Li … Lee?"

"Yep. Now you see why I use an on-air name."

"Not necessarily. Are your first and last names spelled the same?"

"No. My first name is spelled L-I, and my last name is spelled L-E-E."

"Does Li mean anything?"

"I say it means 'pretty powerful.'"

North nodded. "You say that? So, it doesn't really mean that?"

Li relaxed into the conversation. "The name Li can be used for either a boy or a girl. If it's a boy's name, it means 'powerful,' but if it's a girl's name, it means 'pretty.' I prefer to combine the two into one meaning: pretty powerful."

"I love that," North said. "You have a birth name that actually means something to you, and you have given it up for an on-air name that holds no meaning to anybody, but sounds like an old actress. I'd like to take the next few minutes and ask our listening audience to call in and give us their opinion. Should Li make the switch and begin using her given name that has this incredible meaning, or should she stick with Janet?"

Li covered her mouth with her left hand, closed her eyes, and hung her head downward. North knew what she was thinking. Li was afraid of Marcus getting angry, but North had made the decision that if she was indeed going to come back, she had to face her fear of Marcus and eliminate it. She knew she had something to offer the station, and if he wanted to keep it, he had to stop being a bully.

The phone line lit up almost immediately. Li answered, "Hello, WSHS."

"Hi, North!" A woman's voice said. "I'm so glad you're coming back, and I hope you're doing well."

North giggled uneasily. She had forgotten how much she had shared with everyone. "I'm holding it together, thanks for asking."

"Sure thing. And Li?"

"Yeah," Li said.

"I want you to use that beautiful name of yours. I didn't even know you were Asian before this conversation, and I think that's wrong. You say that Janet Leigh is the name of an old actress?"

"Supposedly," Li said.

"Yes, she is," North said. "She's in some Alfred Hitchcock movies."

"Never heard of her. Forget it," the caller said. "You be you, girl!"

North and Li both laughed.

Several more calls came in, and all but one felt that Li should use her given name.

Just then, a shadow appeared in the window and they both looked up to see Marcus standing there with hands on his hips. He was most definitely seething.

"Okay, enough of this," Li said. "We appreciate the calls, but let's get back to the music. Here's one from the early seventies by a one-hit-wonder band called Mouth and MacNeal." She tapped at the screen in front of her and "How Do You Do" began to play.

Marcus walked away from the window, and the rattle of keys could be heard in the lock.

Li snarled at North. "If I get fired for this, I'm going to be so mad at you."

North took in a long, deep breath, hoping to calm the butterflies now taking flight in her stomach. It was not her intention to create trouble for Li. She had just wanted to give her audience the unfiltered "True North" they'd lured back, and Li's name was the first thing that popped into her mind.

The door opened and closed in the small lobby, and a second later, Marcus appeared, filling the doorway to the studio.

"Hi Marcus," Li said. "Look who's back."

Marcus said nothing. He stared at North, red-faced and fire in his eyes.

"Hey, Marcus," North said, trying to sound nonchalant, meanwhile, everything inside her was trembling. "I saw all the signs around town and thought I might give this thing another try."

Marcus stood still with his eyes like lasers glued on North, breathing hard, doing his best to calm down. Eventually, he turned to Li and pointed a puffy finger at her. "You."

North's stomach lurched, and Li's voice cracked when she said, "Yeah?"

"You're no longer Janet on the radio. You're going by Li now."

Li looked over at North, eyes wide with surprise. "Okay, sure. Whatever you say."

Marcus looked back at North, his face less red than it was just a second ago. "And you, Miss Impulsive, I mean—'True North.' Let's go to my office and get a schedule set for your show."

"I could do that," North said, "but I have a question first."

"What's that?" Marcus asked.

"Are *you* going to be real and go by Tony Markum from now on?"

Chapter Fourteen

Marcus refused to go by his real name, and North promised to respect that. However, once he saw the overwhelming support Li received for embracing her real name, his resistance seemed to wane.

After a productive conversation with Marcus, it was agreed upon that North would start back at the radio station three nights a week. Satisfied and excited about the possibilities, North grabbed another hot dog from Chomp's and drove to North Beach. Once parked in the lot off of Lakeshore Drive, she sat on top of the big cement North Beach sign, watching the waves roll in while she ate.

The house Matt had purchased was only one block behind her, so she closed her eyes, took a long, deep breath, and tried to imagine what it would look like to walk down here in the mornings with a steaming hot cup of coffee—to begin her days grounding herself with a stroll in the sand or even dip her feet into the water. She exhaled slowly, and a small smile began to take shape.

After finishing her lunch, North crumpled the cardboard tray in her hand, closed her eyes again, and listened to the water as the cooling breeze blew her sandy blonde hair back. The air smelled clean and felt crisp on her face. North let the moment soothe her soul. She realized this was the calmest she'd felt in weeks.

She now had the peace of mind and newfound curiosity to go check out the house. She tossed her napkin and tray in the trash can and decided to walk up the small incline. People were out on their porches now, and they waved to her as she passed. North waved back through a clenched smile, wondering if they had witnessed her earlier meltdown and were actually praying she wasn't moving in.

Once she reached the house, North stopped in front of it and gave it another long look. She had hoped that in her negative emotional state, she had been too hard on it earlier, but lo and behold, her first impression was deftly accurate. The house was in dire need of a paint job, and given all of the bric-a-brac along the top and edges, that alone would take her all summer to do.

A set of three cement steps led up from the sidewalk to the walkway that ended at the front porch. Though old, they were in good shape, as was the cement walkway. The porch, however, was another story. Years of lake-effect storms had taken their toll, and the whole porch needed to be repainted and perhaps have a few boards replaced.

The door on the front of the house was ornate and surprisingly in beautiful shape, with a sheen that made it appear freshly varnished. At the top, it had a small oval window that North had to stand on her tiptoes to see through. Just above the brass door handle was a business card stuck between the door and the jamb. North pulled it out and flipped it around. It read, "Brax Andrews, Contractor Extraordinaire," and had clip art of hand tools around the edges. She slipped it into her purse, retrieved the key, and tried the lock. It unlatched with ease, and when she turned the handle, the door swung open under its own weight, as if to welcome her inside.

North stepped over the threshold into the foyer of the old house. The first thing she noticed was the smell—a mixture of medicine and musty air. All of the heavy curtains were closed in the house, and not a single light was on, leaving the place dark, even though there wasn't a cloud in the sky.

North threw open the curtain to the right of the door and held her breath. As she backed up, a cloud of dust was illuminated by the sunbeams floating throughout the air.

The foyer was covered in forest green wallpaper, with what appeared to be a busy pattern made of peach-colored irises. The trim was all stained oak, and though dust covered, looked to be in fairly good condition. The same could not be said of the grand wooden staircase, however. The varnish was almost completely worn off the railing and the steps from years of use. Looking up, North noticed an old crystal chandelier. She reached over and flipped the switch to find three of the six bulbs illuminated, giving the dark foyer a little bit of life.

The next room to the right was a formal living room, or a sitting area—whatever they called it at the turn of the last century. A large stone fireplace positioned in the center of the room created a dramatic focal point. The furniture was placed in a formal layout, and every single piece was covered by a dusty tarp. The deep green carpeting was matted and worn threadbare at the entrance to the room and in high traffic areas. This was something that would definitely have to be replaced. Perhaps they would discover a hardwood floor underneath. North smiled at the thought.

The first thing North did was walk over to the front window and open the curtains to let a little daylight in. She wanted to get a better sense of what she was dealing with.

She walked back through the foyer into a dining area with a large wooden table, whose scrapes and stains gave it character, North thought.

Off the dining room was a good-sized kitchen with an island and a door that led to the driveway on the side.

There was a large master bedroom off the foyer, and a smaller room for storage under the stairs.

The second floor had seven rooms, all in varieties of disarray, and on the third floor were four more rooms with a circular stairway that led to the cupola. North wiped at the grime on the windows with her hand to discover a spectacular view of Lake Michigan.

"Hello?"

North faintly heard a woman's voice calling from downstairs. "Just a minute!" she called back.

She ran out of the smelly bedroom and scampered down the stairs to see a woman standing right inside the front door.

The woman saw her and a bright red lipstick smile spread across her face. "Hi there!" She jutted a quick hand in the air to suffice as a wave. "I'm Dietra. Dietra LaRue-Perkins. I own the B&B next door." North made it to the bottom of the stairs and walked up to her with her hand out. "Hi, Dietra LaRue-Perkins. I'm North Nichols-Cooper."

Dietra's handshake was strong, confident, and a bit overpowering. "Pleased to meet you," Dietra said. She looked like she was in her mid-to late-fifties, but was trying very hard to appear in her early thirties. She had big hair with streaks, fifty shades of blonde. Her eyes had been nipped, her chin had been tucked, and her lips were overly puffy, injected with an exorbitant amount of filler. Speaking of overly puffy, her breasts were heaving out of the skin-tight cream camisole she wore under her red blazer, and multiple gold chains were layered across her surgically stretched neck. The entire look was set off by the cream-colored ankle slacks and leopard-print Jimmy Choos.

"What can I do for you?" North asked.

"Not a thing," Dietra said. "I was looking out the front window and saw you walk up and go in, so I thought I'd come over and say, 'welcome to the neighborhood.'" Dietra ended her statement with a wide, but tight-lipped, smile.

North nodded. "Well, thank you. But I'm not sure how long I'll be your neighbor."

"Oh?" Dietra crossed her arms. "Why's that?"

North looked around. "This isn't the type of place I would have chosen for myself."

"Wait a minute," Dietra said. She sounded irritated, but tried her best to cover it by keeping a smile stitched on her face. "There was a bidding war for this place. Someone wanted it awfully badly to drive the price up so high and then pay cash for it."

"How did you know that?"

"Oh, well," Dietra chuckled. "I was going for it, too."

"You wanted this old place?" North asked. "Why?"

"Why?! Because I wanted to turn it into a bed and breakfast. I own three here in South Haven, and I'm also the president of the local Bed and Breakfast Owners Association."

"I see," said North. "Well, I think that's what my husband intended for me to do with the place, but I don't know. There's so much that needs to be done."

"Interesting." Dietra reached up and rubbed her earlobe, feeling the diamond stud. "I actually have plans already drawn up."

"For this place?"

"Mhmm," Dietra nodded, looking away. "I've been waiting years for the old goa … ummm gentleman who lived here to kick … uhhh, finally pass. I was all ready to go, but then I lost the bid."

"I'm sorry," North said.

“Mhmm.” Dietra put her hands on her hips, the sides of her mouth turned down.

“Well, you might just get your chance after all,” North said. “I haven’t decided if I’m going to keep it, and you’ll be the first person I call if I decide to sell.”

“I’d be happy to set up a meeting with my realtor,” Dietra said. “We could probably have the whole thing done as early as tomorrow afternoon.”

“What? No. That won’t work. My husband wouldn’t be able to be here by then, and he has all of the papers on the place. As I said, I have not made any decisions on which way I want to go. I will need some to think on it.”

Dietra nodded. “Okay, then. I’ll be looking forward to hearing from you.” She held out her hand for a shake, which North accepted. Then she turned to walk out the door.

“Oh wait,” North said. “I do have a question.” She pulled the business card that she’d pulled from the front door out of her purse. “Have you heard of a Brax Andrews?”

“Brax? Yes, he’s a contractor. Why?”

“Is he any good?”

Dietra turned back and crossed her arms again. “Why are you asking about a contractor?”

North looked around and waved the card. “Oh, I don’t know. If I did decide to make a go of this, I just would want …”

“You just said you were thinking about selling,” Dietra said, clearly irritated now. “Did you just say that to jerk me around?”

North paused, surprised by the woman’s sudden change in demeanor. “No, not at all. I’m sorry about the confusion. Look, I’m facing a bit of a life crisis these days, and I’m trying to figure things out. My life feels so overwhelming right now, that I don't want to make any hasty decisions and …"

Dietra put her hand up as if to say stop and chuckled, working hard to push her irritation back down. "I'm sorry. I was just surprised by the question." She reached out and put a gentle hand on North's arm. "Look, I'm sorry you're going through such a difficult time right now, but a bed and breakfast is a massive commitment. Talk about overwhelming!" She rolled her eyes and let out a loud laugh. "It's not really an area where someone could just try to figure things out. Trust me when I tell you to run away from this place as fast as you can, hon, and sell it to someone who knows what to do with it."

Different town, same type of person, North thought. Dietra was the kind of person who befriended you, not to be a friend, but only for their own selfish needs. When they realized those needs might not be met, they'd be fine with being your *frenemy*. "Thanks for the advice."

"Any time," Dietra said, flashing her million-dollar smile. "If you need anything at all, just let me know. I'm right next door." She turned to leave once again.

"So, Brax Andrews?" North asked again.

Dietra flipped her tresses back. "What's that?"

"Is Brax Andrews a good contractor? I'm a big reviews and word-of-mouth girl."

Dietra fixed her smile and winked. "He's the only man I call." Then, she pushed open the big wooden door and let herself out, closing it a little harder than one would expect. "Oops," she said on the other side. "Heavy door." "Right, sorry not sorry," said North to no one in particular.

North listened to Dietra's steps fade away and turned back to take one more look. "Matthew, what on earth have you done to me?"

Chapter Fifteen

The loud chirping of the robins in the tree just outside her window woke North. They had no consideration for the sanctity of a good night's sleep. North covered her head with her pillow and tried her best to ignore them for as long as she could, but it was no use. Their high-pitched trill sliced right through her head, letting her know that night was over and it was time to start the day.

North yawned and sat up in bed to stretch, cursing the little buggers under her breath. Then she realized it was Sunday, and the butterflies that had been dancing in her stomach all week began another performance. Today would be the first day of her *new* radio show, where she was now "True North" and people would be listening to her, not for the music she played, but for the thoughts she had to share. The realization made her both anxious and slightly nauseous. She felt a strong desire to aim her blowhorn app at the robins to scare them into silence, then crawl back under the warm covers and stay there until the world faded away.

Just then, like Jiminy Cricket, Aunt El's voice echoed through her conscious. "*The choice is yours, North. Just like the power is yours. Nobody else's.*"

North rolled her eyes. "Thank you, Obi-Wan." She tossed the covers aside, climbed out of bed, and walked over to the window. "Okay, I'm up. You can shut up now."

The robins continued to chirp away merrily.

North grunted and shuffled into the bathroom, splashed water on her face, applied some tinted moisturizer, brushed her teeth, and pulled her hair back into a ponytail. Making breakfast for El was the first item on her agenda, but when she opened her door to head to the kitchen, she was hit with a heavenly aroma.

Aunt El was already up, whipping up breakfast delights in the kitchen. Scrambled eggs with scallions, sausage patties, and the smell of freshly baked biscuits made North's stomach growl loudly.

Aunt El looked up and smiled. "Good morning."

North froze and looked around. The walls were plastered with the papers and posters from around town with the words, 'True North, Come Back!' written all over them. "What's all this?"

"Oh, do you like my redecorating?" Aunt El giggled. "I rather think it makes it much more inviting in here, don't you think?"

North looked at her adopted aunt, the amazing woman who was always in her corner, and her eyes grew watery. "What did I ever do to deserve someone like you in my life?"

El smiled and continued to stir the egg mixture. "I could say the exact same thing, lovely girl. Now have a seat, breakfast is ready."

North saw that the table had already been set with a glass of orange juice and a small dish with a mix of cantaloupe and fresh strawberries waiting for her. "I thought we agreed that I would be making breakfast for you?" She sat down and skewered a piece of melon and strawberry together on her fork, popping the perfect pairing into her mouth.

El was busy plating the main course. "Not today. It's a big day for you, so it's important to start out with a proper breakfast." She stepped in front of North and set down a hot cup of coffee and a plate containing two picture-perfect sausage biscuits sitting next to another strawberry sliced into the shape of a rose, garnished with a mint leaf.

"Aunt El, this looks amazing."

El kissed her on the top of the head. "Good. Then, you're all set for an amazing day."

"Am I?" North looked up at her, while El grabbed her own coffee and plate. "I mean, sure, they wanted me to come back, but that was based on one stupid day that I completely lost my mind on the air. What if I can't be that person again? Will they start posting signs around town that say, 'True North, Go away?'"

El sat next to her with her food and coffee. "And what if they love you, just for who you are? What if they can't get enough of you and want you on the air every single day?"

"I doubt that."

"Don't," El said. "Don't doubt that. Imagine that. Believe in that. Trust in that. But never doubt you or what you have to offer the world, because, sweetie, I'm here to tell you that what you have to offer is substantial, and it won't be long until the world wonders what they ever did without you."

North smiled.

"Now, eat your breakfast and don't say another word, unless it has something to do with manifesting how great you're going to do today."

North finished her breakfast in silence, not because she couldn't imagine being good on the radio, but because she thought she would cry. No one in her life had ever believed in her or treated her as well as Aunt El—not her husband, not her father, and certainly not her mother—but the woman sharing the breakfast table not only loved her but was constantly demonstrating it. North struggled not to be completely overwhelmed by it.

The rest of the day was spent doing some light cleaning and trying to come up with the proper sign-off line. *Be true? Be real? Be truly real? Be really true? Gaaaah*! Nothing sounded right. Perhaps she would borrow the work of one of the greats and go with Shakespeare's 'To thine own self be true.' That line had worked great in a Reba McEntire song, after all

The day zoomed by and before North knew it, it was time for her to go. At 4:45 p.m., she walked through the door of the station, her stomach performing somersaults, as Marcus met her in the studio. "You ready to go, kid?"

"Sure," North said, hoping her fake smile was fooling him.

"I got you something." Marcus pulled a Best Buy bag out of his office and handed it to her.

North looked into the bag and saw a set of Sennheiser headphones still in their cellophaned box. "Thank you," she said.

"Sure thing. Those are yours to keep, so you don't have to use someone else's. You know, ear hygiene, and all."

Marcus unplugged the studio pair and set them off to the side. Once North had hers opened, he took them from her and showed her where to insert them. "One last surprise before I get out of your hair and let you do your show." He pointed to one of the purple boxes on the Arrakis screen that read, "True North Show Open."

"What's that?"

"It's an intro for your show. I made it myself." He smiled at her proudly, both hands tucked into his pants pockets.

"Thank you," she said. "About my show …"

"What about it?"

"I just want to clarify. I can say what I want?"

"Whatever you want, within FCC guidelines."

"Oh, sure. And I can play whatever music I want?"

"Carte blanche."

Marcus stayed in the studio while North got ready, eagerly awaiting her reaction to his intro.

A McDonald's ad finished, and the clock ticked over to 5:00 p.m. The twangy guitar sounds of Depeche Mode rang out, with Marcus's voiceover, "It's now time to get real." Then Depeche Mode sang their lines, "It's too late to change events / it's time to face the consequence / for delivering the proof / in the policy of truth," followed by Marcus's voice again, "And here is your True North host ... North Nichols!"

The music began to fade out, and North hit the button to turn on her mic. "Hello, South Haven. I'm finally back, for real." She looked up at Marcus, who smiled and held up his thumb. She gave him a thumbs-up, and he walked out. This is 'True' North Nichols, and apparently, we have a policy of truth on this show. So, let's get this truth party started. If you're ready to share the truth of your life, please call in now. Until then, here's 'Til Tuesday with "Voices Carry."

She hit the play button on the screen, and then tapped her mic off. North smiled as she thought how Marcus's open was actually quite clever, so she typed 'truth' into the search field to find more songs that fit the theme. Her eyes widened as several came up. Like a kid in a candy store, she began to scroll through and hit 'select' to populate her playlist with artists like John Lennon, Jason Aldean, and James Blunt. Then the station hotline rang.

She jumped, but had previously considered how she would answer the phone. "WSHS, what's your truth?"

"No," the woman's voice on the phone said. "We want to know what *your* truth is."

"What do you mean?"

"When you last went off the air, you shared with us that your husband had left you for a man. How is that whole situation? Are you back together? Are you divorced? What's going on?"

"Well, that's not what this is about," North said. "I don't want the focus to be all about me. I'm hoping to get a conversation started about someone else's issues. Do you have anything you want to share?"

"No, but …"

"Then I'm going to take another caller." North tapped off the call and almost immediately, the phone rang again. "WSHS, what's your truth?"

"Welcome back, North," a woman said.

"Thank you."

"So, how has everything been going?" she asked. "When we last heard, your life was falling apart. How is that all coming along?"

North scoffed. "Forget about me. What about you? Don't you have anything you want to share?"

"No, I'm good."

"Then I'm going to have to take another caller." Again, she hung up before the caller had a chance to respond and answered another. "Do you have a truth to share?"

"Nah, girl," a man's voice said. "I just wanted to know how you were doing."

"It's not about me," North said, ending the call abruptly.

More lines began to light up, but North was afraid to answer them. She tapped the table anxiously with her fingers. This show was going off the rails before she even had a chance to get it going. She didn't want to sit around and cry to everyone about her problems anymore. She was no longer in the same mood she was the first time she had been on-air. Now, she wanted to be able to make a difference in the lives of other people. She had no interest in hosting a show that would revolve entirely around her life, her problems, essentially her dirty laundry, day after day.

As "Voices Carry" ended, North made a decision to right the ship. She turned on the microphone and spoke with her most cheerful voice, "Hello, and a good Sunday afternoon to you. I've taken a few calls, but they were all just questions about me. I want you to know that I appreciate the interest, I really do, but I want to talk about you! This is your station, and I want to provide you with a platform to talk about the things going on in your lives. What are your challenges, your issues? What are the truths that you're struggling to face? The lines are all open, so give me call. Maybe this song from the great John Lennon will provide you with a little inspiration, a little courage, or both!" North hit 'play,' and John Lennon began belting out his angsty tune "Gimme Some Truth."

Twenty seconds later, the phone lit up. "WSHS—Gimme some truth." North giggled, thinking herself quite clever.

"You first," came the young woman's voice on the line.

"No." North shook her head. "I just explained that this show isn't supposed to be about me."

"But you can't do that," the voice said.

"I can't do what?"

"You can't come back on the air and then drop everything that made us like you in the first place. It's like a bait and switch. Why should we even listen to you now?"

"Okay," North quipped. "I'll bite. Why *should* you listen to me?"

"We wanted you to come back because we wanted to know what's going on with you," the girl said. "You invited us all into your life, made us care, and now we want to be a part of it. We don't want to just listen to a bunch of random people complaining about their problems."

"You want to just listen to me complaining about mine? Does it make you feel better about yourself if I tell you that my life is shit?"

North heard the girl sigh. "Never mind," she said. And then she hung up.

"Hello?"

North gritted her teeth and tapped the call off. Two more lines were waiting to be answered.

North tapped the first one. "WSHS."

"Yo," a young man's voice said. "If you're not going to talk, can you at least play something from this century?"

North tapped off the call, pulled her brand new Sennheiser headphones off her head, slammed them on the counter and screamed, "Gaaaaaaah!" Then she turned to the Arrakis, deleted all of the songs she had just brought into the playlist, erased her search, and queued up "So What" by Pink.

For the remainder of her shift, North didn't answer one more phone call. She kept her talk to a minimum, only turning on the mic when it was time to give the weather updates.

Shaking her head, she turned on her cell phone and started aggressively tapping her screen, scrolling through job recruiting sites. After tonight, it was crystal clear that her career in radio was going to be filed under the same category of her life as marriage: "F" for "Fail."

Chapter Sixteen

North awoke the next morning and got out of bed when the robin's song beckoned. Interestingly, she no longer felt like hiding away. In fact, she felt well rested and ready to take on the day. The previous evening's radio debacle had put her in a completely different frame of mind, and after Aunt El had delivered her powerful tough love speech, she certainly couldn't face her now and act like the victim playing the 'poor me' card. On the contrary, she was going to start steering her own ship, just like El had advised her to do. Matthew had purchased her a house and she needed to investigate whether turning it into a business opportunity or unloading it for cash was the better option.

With the sun shining brightly, June was starting out to be quite the warm month in South Haven, so she threw on some running shorts, a sports bra, and tank top, and headed to the kitchen. She quickly whipped up a batch of lemon-blueberry pancakes with a side of extra crispy bacon, and enjoyed a nice, quiet breakfast with Aunt El. North was grateful that El never mentioned a word about her show, and she wasn't about to bring it up. Some things are best swept under the rug.

After doing the dishes and cleaning the kitchen, North made a beeline back to her room, grabbed her purse, and pulled out the business card she had retrieved from the door of the house. She pulled out her phone and dialed the "Contractor Extraordinaire." The phone rang twice, and then a deep male voice answered, "This is Brax."

"Oh, hi, Mr. Andrews. My name is North Nichols. I believe you left your card on the porch of my house on Grand Boulevard."

"Did I?" the man said with a chuckle. "I do that an awful lot."

"Well, my husband bought me the house thinking I might like to turn it into a bed and breakfast, so I was wondering if you could come by to give me some estimates."

"I'm on a job site for most of today," Brax said, "but I could cut loose a little early. Would four p.m. work for you?"

"Oh, sure." North had hoped it would be sooner, but perhaps there were some simple things she could begin to do herself.

"Now, which house are we talking about?"

"It's 21 East Grand Boulevard."

"Wait," Brax said. "Isn't that Dietra LaRue's place? If memory serves, she told me to be ready because she would be getting the keys to that place soon."

"Hmmm," North scowled and pursed her lips together tightly. She remembered telling Dietra she *might* sell it, but she never committed to her pushy new neighbor. "It's actually my place. I haven't yet decided if it will or it won't be Dietra's, or anyone else's, for that matter. I guess a lot of that will depend on our conversation at four o'clock."

"Huh. Okay," Brax said. "This could get interesting." He chuckled again and added, "I'll see you at four," then hung up the phone.

North pulled the phone away from her ear and looked at it to make sure the call was indeed over. She now had another item on her to-do list—have an uncomfortable conversation with Dietra.

After making a grocery list of some basic cleaning essentials, she jumped in her car and drove over to Meijer to make her purchases: a bucket, sponges, Dawn dish soap, Clorox Wipes, paper towels, glass cleaner, a broom, dust pan, garbage bags, a six-pack of Diet Coke, a six-pack of Bell's Two-Hearted Ale, a bag of ranch-flavored Doritos, and two cream-filled long johns. The last two items were food that would help her power through the day.

Parking her Impreza in the driveway, North discovered a side door that led directly into the kitchen. She took the food in first, putting the Cokes and beer in the refrigerator. When she headed back out, there was Dietra dressed in a very revealing, bright pink camisole, and gray Lululemon yoga pants, walking quickly toward her. She was obviously on a mission.

"Good morning," she said, with a high-pitched voice and fake, toothy smile.

"Good morning," North said, reaching into the car and grabbing the bucket full of cleaning supplies.

"I saw you stop in and thought I'd come over to see what was going on. I hadn't heard from you or a real estate agent about selling the property." Dietra stopped when she saw the bucket, and the smile evaporated from her face. "What's going on?"

"Nothing, really," North said with a shrug. "I'm just not sure I'm there yet."

"Where yet?" Dietra asked, a much less-friendly tone in her voice now.

"I'm not sure I'm at the selling point yet. I'm still trying to figure this life thing out. I guess I want to explore a bit and find out exactly what this might entail."

Dietra let out a laugh. "Oh, sweetheart. A place like this isn't for someone who's trying to figure her life out. An endeavor this complicated is a commitment."

"Well," North said, "to be honest, I think I just might be looking for this kind of commitment. I'll have to see."

"But wait, I don't understand." Dietra put her hands on her hips. "When I spoke with you before, you had talked about just unloading this place. What changed?"

"Life. Circumstances. Outlook." North shrugged a shoulder. "All of it, I guess. I have a guy stopping by later today to talk with me about what it would take to convert this place into a B&B."

"A guy?" Dietra asked. "Do you mean Brax?"

"Yes. He's coming over this afternoon. In the meantime, I thought I'd start with a bonding-through-cleaning exercise to try to get more familiar with the place." North turned and climbed the two steps to the door. "So, I'm going to go ahead and get started." She turned and smiled. "It was good to see you again, Dietra. Have a good day."

Dietra said nothing back. She just stood there, looking like she'd been slapped.

North headed inside and closed the door behind her, then peered out through the curtains.

Dietra spun around and stormed back to her house next door.

"Not sure that could have been more awkward," North said under her breath. She dropped the bucket, pulled one of the long johns out of the bag, and took a big bite.

She pulled one of the Diet Cokes out of the fridge, popped it open, and took a deep swig. She finished her second breakfast staring out the window at the little glimpse of beach she could see between two houses across the street from her.

When she was done eating, she put the rest of the Coke back in the fridge to finish cooling and began taking inventory. The kitchen itself was quite large, albeit not that modern. The ceiling was quite high, though, which allowed for very tall cabinets. An old yellowed wallpaper border ran the entirety of the ceiling, featuring chickens, grapes, tomatoes, frying pans, and copper kettles.

The stove, though old, had four well-used gas burners. North turned one on, and it fired up right away. It needed to be scrubbed, but it looked like it could stay until she had money for a new one.

The oven underneath still worked as well, but it was going to take significantly more work. The drippings on the bottom and splatters on the sides and door were layered from years of use.

North opened all of the cupboards and pulled all of the dinnerware, glasses, bowls, and pans out. There was a substantial amount, although not much of it matched. She wondered if that would be considered quaint or crap in the B&B world.

She put in her earbuds, turned on Spotify on her phone, and filled the bucket with Dawn and hot water. Then, she spent the day cleaning every surface, corner, nook, and cranny in the entire kitchen, stopping only now and again to grab another Diet Coke and a handful of Doritos. Around two o'clock, she washed her hands, grabbed the other long john, and walked out to the backyard to enjoy it.

This was a treasure that she hadn't bothered to see the first time she had visited the house. It had a beautiful porch made of red paving brick with a large fire pit in the center, and was closed in on all three sides by pine trees and bushes that offered plenty of privacy. The lawn was broken up by five raised garden beds, which were mostly full of weeds at this point, but North could see the remnants of tomato and cucumber plants in a couple of them. There was a water feature in one corner of the yard, and a small gazebo in the other, with Edison lights strung between that and the house.

North sat in a beautiful Adirondack chair whose back was shaped like the Mitten State and ate her lunch. She stared at the gazebo, picturing this space in the evening—guests sitting out under the lights, drinking local Michigan wines and eating blueberry pie made from locally grown blueberries, with some musician and their acoustic guitar, belting out old Janis Joplin tunes. In fact, North would demand Janis Joplin.

In that moment, North decided that she was going to make this place into the best B&B South Haven had to offer. This house could eventually mean North's freedom, and as Janis had said, "Freedom's just another word for nothing left to lose."

She spent the remainder of the afternoon pulling weeds from the garden beds. The beds on the ends had flowers in them, and she tried her best to salvage them, while simultaneously freeing them from the strangling weeds.

Around 3:30 p.m., North was growing nervous about what Brax would say about her plans. She grabbed a beer and another handful of Doritos and sat in the front window, waiting.

Four o'clock came and went with no Brax. She felt like calling him, but wanted to drink a little more courage first. She grabbed another beer and told herself that if he hadn't shown by the time she was done with her chips, she would call him. The can of beer was running low when a powder-blue pickup truck pulled up out front with a sign on the side that said, "Brax's got your back!"

The driver got out, and North choked on her beer. The man was a blonde, tanned god. He looked down at his smudged sleeveless t-shirt and decided to change it. He pulled it up over his head, revealing a perfectly sculpted chest and a set of abs that you could do laundry on.

He reached into his truck, pulled out another t-shirt and threw it on, stretching it over his muscled frame. Then he sauntered, John Wayne style, up to her front door.

North watched every step, lost in the absolute beauty of this man. When the knock came at the door, she jumped, sloshing beer down the front of her shirt. "Shit," she said, trying in vain to wipe away the wet stain. She ran into the kitchen, grabbed a paper towel, and tried to sop it up. Another knock came at the door, and she gave up. "Coming."

She hurried to the front door and opened it. Brax stood with his back to her, looking out at the neighborhood and the water. He spun and gave her a sly smile, making dimples in his tanned cheeks. "Hi, I'm Brax."

North didn't recall a time when she had looked at a man this gorgeous. She was dumbstruck. With a nervous wave, North responded, "Hi, I'm Brax … ummm. No. You're Brax. I'm not." She let out an awkward giggle.

He chuckled and held out his hand. "Well, now that we know that only one of us is named Brax, what did you say your name was?"

"North." She grabbed his hand and shook it vigorously. "I'm North."

Brax looked confused. "Is that really your name?"

"Yep."

"North? Like, the opposite of south?"

"Yep, that's me."

"I like it. It's a unique name."

"So's Brax."

"It's short for Braxton."

"Oh." North stood in the doorway, taking in the looks and the charm of the man in front of her.

After an awkward moment, he nodded at her. "Did you still want me to look at the place for you?"

"Oh, why yes." She feigned a cough and stepped aside. "Come on in."

"No worries." He stepped in and immediately his head darted along the ceiling, to the walls, and then down to the floor. "Huh," he muttered, then wandered into the living room, eyes scanning every inch of the place. "Hmmm."

Though North enjoyed looking at the man, she didn't enjoy the sound of his mutters. They resembled the sounds of the Meijer cash-only self-checkout lane and amped her anxiety. "Can I get you a beer?" She thought things might go better for both of them if she loosened him up a bit.

He rapped on the mantle with his knuckles and bent down to look into the fireplace. "Sure."

She slipped into the kitchen, and grabbed two cold beers out of the fridge. She handed him one when she returned.

"Woman after my own heart," he said with his killer smile.

"Pardon?"

"Bell's is my go-to." He took the beer from her, popped the top, and took a long drink.

North did the same.

Brax wiped his mouth with the back of his hand. "So, tell me about yourself, North."

She swallowed, almost choking. She coughed a little and then managed, "What would you like to know?"

"Oh, I don't know." He shrugged. "Where are you from, and how'd you end up with a hundred-plus-year-old home down here in South Haven?"

"Oh. Well. My husband bought this house for me as a surprise."

Brax glanced over at her. "Husband, huh?"

"Umm … ex- … soon-to-be ex-husband … I guess."

Brax picked at the seam of the wallpaper. "Sounds complicated."

"It is and it isn't. He found someone he likes better than me, so he's moving on."

Brax looked back at her. "He's a dumb shit, if you ask me," he said, punctuating his statement with a wink and a dimpled smile.

North felt the heat of her blush. "Thank you."

"He bought you this house as a consolation prize or something?"

"Something like that. I suppose he wanted to ease his guilt, as well as distract me from the fact that my life and future dreams were crashing down around me." She took a long drink from her beer in order to keep from oversharing and looking completely pathetic.

"I see," Brax said. He took another long drink from his own beer. "So, you want to convert this place into a bed and breakfast?"

"That's the thought, anyway. Do you think it can be done?"

"Oh, sure." Brax said, "but we need to determine exactly what your vision is before I can give you any kind of a quote." He gestured to the sofa. "Any chance we can get a couple more of these and discuss the plan?"

North grabbed the last two beers and sat with Brax on the sofa. He made a toast to her "possibilities," then launched into an explanation of what he believed had to happen up front, like a small office space near the front door to check guests in and out, disperse keys, etc. Since a room didn't exist for that, he would have to adjust walls to build it.

"I have to be honest, I'm a little nervous here," he said almost shyly. "I don't want to say so much that I scare you away."

"Don't want to lose my business?" North asked.

"Don't want to lose the chance at getting to know you," he said, before looking down at his notes.

"Oh," North smiled and blushed again. "Why isn't there a Mrs. Brax?"

He chuckled, took a swig of his beer, and looked down at the can in his hand. "I guess, because I'm basically married to my job and my clients, this line of work doesn't leave me with a lot of room for a personal life."

North nodded and let it go.

"Sheesh, I don't know." Brax ran a hand up through his hair and looked up at her. "I got a call from Dietra this morning telling me if I were to give you some outrageous quote to scare you off, that I would get a big job out of this place, and she would make it worth my while. But after meeting you, I've decided not to." His blue eyes looked straight into hers and he spoke with a low and serious tone. "I'll tell you what, North. If you decide to stay here, we can take this job as slow as you want, and I can make it all worth *your* while."

North's jaw dropped open as she caught her breath, and she almost spilled her beer. With her heart racing, she licked her lips and allowed herself be completely engulfed by the feelings she was now experiencing. It had been a long time since she had felt wanted. Her whole body tingled with desire, and she wasn't going to fight it. She downed the rest of her beer, slammed the can down on the table next to her, and lunged forward toward Brax. He caught her in his arms, as if he were expecting her to do just that. He swung her around, cradled her in his arms, and kissed her hungrily.

North was overcome by his desire. It felt good—no it felt euphoric—to be wanted, especially by this gorgeous man. As he began to kiss her neck and fondle her breast, she fell completely under his spell. With an animal-like hunger, she clawed at his fresh shirt and pulled it up over his head. His breath was hot and his breathing rapid as he reached down to pull her top up over her head. His mouth and tongue followed, and she groaned with desire. She was glad she had worn her cute lace bra that fastened in the front. Brax smiled up at her right before he unfastened it with his teeth and began to explore her breasts with his tongue. North cried out, "Take me, dammit!"

The rest of the afternoon was a heavenly blur. They enjoyed each other twice before collapsing, sweaty and exhausted, in each other's arms.

For North it was more than just sex, it was validation that she was still a desirable woman with something to offer. It was also the first time in her life where she hadn't planned or thought about the possible consequences of her actions. She simply went with her feelings, and right now, it felt amazing to be a woman.

Chapter Seventeen

"What's up with you, girl?" Aunt El asked. "You're acting strange this morning."

"Strange how?" North said.

"I don't know," El said. "You're just in too good of a mood. It seems a little suspicious to me."

North had been singing silly little songs and humming all morning while she made breakfast. Aunt El looked at her like she had sprouted wings or something.

"Hmmm, I don't know," North said. "I guess I'm choosing to be more positive."

"Well don't get me wrong, child, I like the new you. I just didn't expect to wake up to this much … joy." She took a sip of her coffee. "You must really be looking forward to your radio show this evening."

North scoffed. "Not one bit. But that doesn't mean the day is a total loss, does it?"

Aunt El clicked her tongue. "I guess not." She downed the last of her coffee in one gulp and stood. "Well, I have several errands to run today. If I don't see you, have a great show tonight."

"Thanks, Aunt El." North did the dishes and cleaned up the kitchen, then ran into her room, pulled out her phone, and dialed Matthew.

"Hey, North," he said. "How are things going?"

"Well," North said, hardly able to contain herself. "I have some news."

"Oh? What is it?"

"I'm pretty sure that I cheated on my husband yesterday."

"What? You did?" There was a slight pause and then, "Congratulations."

North rolled her eyes when she realized how twisted this conversation was. Why the hell did she feel she needed to let Matt know? Then again, why the hell not? In all fairness, besides his sister, he was the one person she confided everything in—and if he could step out, why not her?

"That's terrific," he said. "With who?"

North's chin dropped open. Did he have to be so happy about it? Couldn't he at least be the slightest bit upset, or was he so over her that he didn't care what she did anymore or who she did it with?

She felt the heat rise on her neck and realized she no longer wanted to talk to him. "Just this guy I met. Anyway, I thought you ought to know. I gotta go now."

"Okay," Matthew said. "Well, I'm happy for you."

"Yeah, thanks."

"And, North?"

"What?"

There was a pause before Matt said, "Just so you know, I would be lying if I said I wasn't just a little bit jealous."

North was silent.

"Okay, bye," he said.

"Bye," North said. Once the call went dead, she looked at her phone for a moment and began screaming, "You fickle piece of shit! Why would you say that to me?"

North ran into the bathroom and splashed cool water on her face, then looked in the mirror at the drowned rat staring back at her and scolded herself, "What did you expect, dumb-ass? Why would he be the first one you shared this with? He's not your friend. He's about to be your *ex*-husband. If you're really going to move on, then move *on*."

She put on her tennis shoes, grabbed her phone and her earbuds, and headed out the door for a long, draining run. She chose a route that was farther and more difficult than she had run in a very long time, but she pushed herself, as if this was the only way to outrun the shreds of her life.

When she got back home, she grabbed a bottle of water and headed to the backyard, where she collapsed into one of the blue Adirondack chairs near the flower bed. She needed to get centered and change her thoughts so she turned her attention to the radio show she was scheduled to do that night. It was time to make a decision. Was she going to present herself as True North, or was she going to be just another DJ on the air playing happy hits?

Just for fun, she pulled out her phone and Googled "How to do a radio talk show," as if, like a crystal ball, that would give her some clear ideas on what to do. Then surprisingly, up popped a seven-step process for hosting an actual radio talk show. Step one was 'Know your listener.'

North raised her eyebrows, took a deep breath, and realized she hadn't given that any thought. She had somehow made a connection to her audience the first time she was on the air, and they had responded so strongly that they had wanted her back; but she hadn't even tried to connect the next time. Instead, she'd just expected that since she'd come back, they would chime in exactly like they had done the first time. There was no topic or direction, so the audience had called in asking about her. What they really needed was for North to take the reins and direct the conversation.

Step two was, 'Make the listener care.' Again, she had done that the first time without even trying. Her listeners cared about the scenario she had presented to them. The fact that it happened to be about her was just the way the conversation had played out. It literally could have been about anyone, she realized.

Perhaps this time, she could give them more of what they wanted. She could begin by making it about herself just long enough to get them on the hook, then she could spin it around to make it about them.

This could actually be fun ... if it worked.

Feeling more hopeful, North got up and stretched her arms up over her head, then headed back inside the house. She took a steaming hot shower, put on a little make-up (something she hadn't done in a awhile), and grabbed a copy of an old Elin Hilderbrand book off Aunt El's bookshelf. Smiling to herself, North grabbed a glass of iced tea with a slice of lime and headed back out to the flower garden for a much-needed escape to Nantucket Island. She would indulge herself in the delicious fictional drama all afternoon until it was time to go to work.

North arrived early at WSHS to get herself prepared for the evening's discussion. She wanted to search through all of the truth-themed songs again and insert them back into the playlist.

Li had the Tuesday afternoon shift and was finishing up her show while North worked from the other seat. "You have an unusual glow about you," Li said.

North smiled and continued to stare at the screen. "Do I?"

"Wait," Li slapped her hand on the table. "Did you get laid?"

North giggled. "Oh, my god. Is it that obvious?"

"Congrats," Li said. "You're starting to move on with your life." She gave North a high five. "So, give me the juicy deets. Who was he … or she …?"

"It was a he," North said. "I know it sounds really cliché and all, but it was the hottest contractor you have ever seen in your life."

"A *contractor*?"

"Mm hmm."

"Wait," Li looked concerned. "Please tell me it wasn't Brax Andrews?"

North's eyes doubled in size. "Wait—what? How did you know that?"

Li looked up at the ceiling. "Because that's his M.O. He finds an older woman that smells of desperation and takes advantage of her."

"Hold on. This is a regular thing he does?"

"Yep. He's got a reputation around town. The majority of his clients are repeat customers—mostly old, rich women who need a hot contractor to do some … servicing."

North was having a hard time hiding her disappointment. "So, he wasn't really into me like he said he was?"

"Oh, I'm sure he was into you," Li said. "You're much younger and prettier than the majority of his clients. But, I'm also sure he's not your long-term Mr. Right, if that's what you were hoping. Did you see the slogan on his truck?"

"'Brax's got your back?'"

"Yeah. His buddies razz him, saying that it should actually say, 'Brax *gets* you on your back.'"

"How do you know all this? Did he … service you?"

"Hell no," Li shook her head. "Not that I would let him if he wanted to," she chuckled. "I mean OMG, right?"

North pressed her lips tightly together.

"He graduated high school two years ahead of me, so he's been kicking around this town a long time. It's not that big of a town, so word definitely gets around."

North nodded and quietly said, "Thanks."

"Oh, shit, I'm sorry," Li said. "I didn't mean to dim your glow; I'm just trying to look out for you."

North held up a hand and shook her head. "No worries. I appreciate that. I did have a good time, and that's how I need to look at it." She went back to work on the Arrakis. "Thanks for having my back."

Li said nothing more for the next few minutes and let North go quietly about her business.

All niceties aside, North began silently seething about being played by such a manipulative sleazeball. It now became obvious that he'd told her about Dietra trying to run her out of town to gain her trust, then continued his bait with, "I don't want to say too much so that I scare you away," and "Don't want to lose the chance getting to know you." If all of that wasn't enough, the mere thought of Brax naked with uppity Dietra was enough to make North vomit all over the keyboard.

"He's the only one I call?" North said aloud, trying her best to sound like Dietra with a nasally voice.

"What's that?" Li said.

North looked up and shook her head. "Nothing."

Li put on her headphones and turned on her microphone, quipping, "That's it for me today. I'll be turning things over to our own True North right after the Thompson Twins. Peace." She pressed a button and "King for a Day" started playing.

Li gathered up her bottle of water and half empty package of peanuts and stood. "Try to have a good night."

North nodded. "Thanks, I'll do my best." She took her seat in the main chair, and Li left the building, stopping to give her a peace sign as she passed by the window out front.

When the Thompson Twins finished, Marcus's recorded open for True North played, then she tapped on her mic. "Hi Friends! I hope you've left your judgments at the office and are feeling open-minded, because tonight our journey of truth takes us to a topic not frequently discussed: the hookup. Yes, you heard me I said the hookup, and I don't mean giving a car a jump start. So, tell me, what does it mean to you? Is it just mindless sex or is there something more? I want to be very clear though—I'm not talking about a monogamous agreement, and I'm certainly not talking any kind of sexual abuse or assault. I'm talking purely consensual here, whether you were on the same page emotionally, or not. Because, the thing is, I may or may not have had a hookup recently and, well, I just need some advice. Give it some thought and call in if you have some truth you'd like to share with me—only please remember to keep it as PG as possible." She tapped 'play' on George Michael's "I Want Your Sex," then tapped off her microphone and let out an audible exhale. "Well, here we go," she murmured to herself.

The phone lit up immediately. "True North here, can I put you on the air?"

"Sure," said the woman on the other end of the line. "So, are we to assume that you have officially moved on?"

"I don't think anybody should ever *assume* anything."

"Touché. However, if you're having sexual relations, doesn't that demonstrate that you're moving ahead with your life?"

"Hmmm. Not that I'm going to kiss and tell, but what if I did?" North asked. "Should it have meant something to me or not?"

The woman sighed and clicked her tongue. "I guess I'm just too old-fashioned. I naturally assume that if someone willingly engages in sexual relations, then there must be a relationship."

"Hm, I think there was a time I may have thought that, too," North said, "but what if I just needed it as a way to help heal the hurt? What then?"

"Hmm … well, I really don't know. I'll let you chat with someone else regarding that." Then she hung up.

Three other lines were lighting up. "This is True North and we're talking right now about having sex to heal a hurt. Good thing or bad thing?"

"Am I, like, on the air?" a young woman asked.

"You are."

"Oh cool! So, like rebound sex? Like, how can that *ever* be bad? You're like, getting over something, so you work out your hurt with sex. Isn't that like, healthy?"

"I don't know, is it?"

"Like, yeah!"

"But what if that's all it is for one person, but the other person actually has feelings?"

"Oh … that sucks. Then it gets, like, complicated."

"Exactly."

The evening seemed to be going better than she had imagined it would. Calls were coming in faster than she could answer them, and unlike her previous show, everyone appeared to be engaged in the topic. Everyone has opinions about sex.

North heard stories about breakup sex, one-night stands, losing bets, winning bets, and even a story about an unnamed contractor who enjoyed a little more deck action than expected, all of which helped North ease into the topic she really wanted to discuss. "Okay! Now that we've talked about the hookup, let's go deeper into the weeds and talk about that elusive thing called love," she said. " More specifically, how does it actually develop? If we catch feelings for someone, is there a way to make it reciprocal—say, through our words and behaviors? Once someone professes their love for us, how do we know that it's real, and most importantly, how do we make it last? To help you ponder those questions, here's Queen with "Crazy Little Thing Called Love."

Hardly seconds had gone by, when several phone lines lit up at once. "You're talking with True North, can I put you on the air?"

"Definitely," said the female on the other end of the line. "Are you seriously asking if we can manipulate someone into falling in love with us? Because if you are, I want to know the answer!"

North laughed at just how ludicrous that sounded aloud. "Then keep listening! Maybe we can find out together."

She tapped the next line and the next, only to hear multiple sad stories of lost loves and excitement to find out the answers to her questions.

When Queen ended, North played a couple of commercials and went straight into another song so she could continue to answer the lines.

"This is True North, do you have an answer?"

"Love just ain't that simple," a male voice said. North could tell he was older by the scratchiness in his tired voice and the slow, methodical way he spoke.

"What do you mean? And with whom am I speaking?"

"This is George. It's just, well, love ain't some recipe you can create with a half cup of this and a tablespoon of that. Friendship, maybe—but not love."

"Keep going," said North.

Just then, a dog started barking in the background, and the man stopped to talk to the dog. "Cupid. Go lay down. It's just a damn squirrel." The dog grunted, then was silent. "Sorry about that," the man said.

"No problem," North said. "Your dog's name is Cupid?"

"Yep," he said. "Cheesy, I know, but I think love is the greatest gift, and nobody ever loves you more than a dog."

"That's very sweet. So, what are your thoughts about sex? Can it lead to love?"

"I don't know. It just seems to me that young people are looking at it in much the same way that we did back in the sixties with the whole "love the one you're with," and all that. I don't think it worked back then, and I can't believe that it's working out now. True love is a mystery. You can't make somebody fall in love with you anymore than you can make them like liver—they either will or they won't, and I think that anyone who tries to create somethin' that doesn't unfold naturally is in for a rude awakening. Oh, you may think that by buying somebody gifts or acting like you're somebody you're not will win someone's heart, but you can only keep that up for so long, and before you know it, the arguments start and the accusations fly, like—I thought you liked liver or sports or whatever it was you faked in order to get what you thought you wanted. My advice is to be true to yourself, and the right one will eventually find you. Of course, you gotta put yourself out there for it to happen. If you're staying home every night watching reality dating shows, well that's all you're going to have."

"So, wait, let me get this straight—are you saying a hookup, or even sex in general, can't lead to love?"

"What I'm saying is, there are men out there who like sex and will do or say just about anything to get it; but there are also men that don't like to have sex unless they have real feelings for the person they're with. You don't hear about it, because they aren't the ones bragging at the top of their lungs, and if they decide to sleep with you, you can be damned sure that their heart is in it. Wise people understand that there's a lot of power in sex, not just for the obvious reasons, but because it can also carry the potential for great love."

This was by far the most interesting person that had been on the entire show. "Well George, you have definitely given us all something to think about. Thank you for your comments—and give Cupid a hug for me."

The man chuckled. "I will."

"We're going to take a little music break here to process this last conversation with Sir Paul McCartney and Wings and 'Silly Love Songs.'"

North took a long drink of her water and started thinking about her own life. She was no longer concerned about Brax Andrews. He was nothing more than an asshole who would never get the chance to touch a single nail on her house. Her thoughts were now on Matthew—specifically, the many times they'd had sex. Those moments were filled with excitement, passion, and pleasure, and she was certain his heart had been in it. What had changed? Did anything change? He said he still loved her.

Then, the seed of an idea began to sprout.

Chapter Eighteen

"Hey beautiful. I was hoping you'd call." Brax even poured on the charm over the phone. It seemed to be second nature to him, especially once he felt he had you ensnared. "When do you want me to start?"

"Well, I need a few questions answered first," North said.

"Sure. Fire away."

"Exactly how loud does Dietra get during her orgasms?"

"What?"

"Yes, and how many other women north of the river have you done contract work for? Oh, and does every job come with a free screw, or is it just those with B&Bs?"

"Hey, listen." Brax was clearly rattled. "I don't know what you've heard, but …"

"Oh, I've heard plenty, Mr. 'Brax gets you on your back.'"

"Come on. You can't tell me you didn't enjoy it. I know I did."

"Perhaps you'll enjoy the notoriety too, because you came up during my radio show last night."

"Radio show?"

"Yeah, *True North*. Ever hear of it?"

There was a short pause before Brax started again. "You're ... True North?"

"Yep."

"And you talked about me ... us, on the radio last night?"

"I didn't. Another one of your conquests did."

"Was it positive or negative?"

North had had enough. "Listen, you piece of shit. This is the last time we're talking. You got that? If you see me walking down the street, look away. In fact, cross the street so I don't have to be anywhere near you. And if you try to talk to me, I will let all of southwest Michigan know what a scumbag you are. Got it?"

"Do that, and I'll sue you for defamation." Brax was trying his best to get his swagger back.

"Give it your best shot, but it's not defamation if it's true, dumbass." She hung up, jumped off her bed and danced around the room in her South Haven t-shirt, panties, and white socks. She stopped in front of the mirror and pointed at her reflection. "You are a badass, and you're taking control of your life." She kissed her reflection, and for the first time in a long time, she was proud of herself.

North was still furious with Brax Andrews. No one wants to be just another conquest, but she had to admit, she was a little bit grateful to him too. He, or rather the experience he'd provided, had given her a direction on her radio show, and the show was a success. She had a string of callers all night long engaging in a very lively discussion. In fact, there had still been callers on the line that she couldn't get to by the end of the show. Sex and love were definitely topics that she'd have to revisit.

However, she couldn't stop thinking about the older caller named George. He had said something that had her head spinning: *There's a lot of power in sex, because it can carry with it the potential for great love.*

She sat back down on the bed and dialed Matthew.

"Hey, North. Good morning."

"Hi, Matthew. I was wondering if you had some time this weekend to come over and see the house."

"I could do that. What's going on?"

"Well, I'm actually considering your idea, you know, to make it into a B&B, and I wanted to run some ideas by you."

"That's great, but you don't need my approval on anything. Just go ahead and do it."

"I know that. I'm not looking for your approval, just your opinion. I don't have anybody else to run ideas by."

"Okay. When do you want to do it?"

"How about Friday evening? You can spend the night. You'll be the first guest at North Haven."

Matthew chuckled. "North Haven?"

"Yeah. That's what I'm thinking of calling it. It's north of the river, just off North Beach and of course … me." North smiled.

"I like it. Alright then, I'll plan on it. See you around 7:30 on Friday."

"Great. Don't eat. I'll have food for us when you get there."

"Sounds good, thanks. See you then." He hung up, and North looked at herself in the mirror, trying to recognize the person she saw. Her intention was to seduce her husband to make him realize the love they truly had for each other, but how was that any better than what Brax Andrews had done to her? She leaned into her reflection to give herself a pep talk: "The difference is you're husband and wife," she said. "Of course you should be able to hook up, have sex, make love, or whatever label you want to place on it. There's nothing wrong with this." She nodded to her reflection and got on with her day.

North got to work making a list of various topics she thought might generate some good discussions on her show—self acceptance, kindness, online dating, separating chemistry from love, finding one's purpose, and maybe throw in a little metaphysics, like astrology or feng shui.

This was a good start. She could always add to the list as time went on, and even allow major current events to steer the conversations. She went back through her list and began to add talking points for each topic. Satisfied with the prep work, she closed her computer.

North then went to ask Aunt El if she could borrow her vacuum. Of course, El had absolutely no problem with it, so she packed up the Dyson and headed back to the house to clean.

She parked out front, pulled the vacuum out of her car, and was just heading up to the front door when she noticed Dietra next door, sitting on her front porch swing, ice-cold beverage in hand, glaring at her.

North stopped and called out, "Honestly, Dietra, I still don't know what I'm going to do about the house, but I might have an answer for you on Saturday."

Dietra's glare softened slightly, and she simply nodded to North, then looked off in the other direction.

North walked up the creaky stairs onto the paint-chipped porch and opened the door. The air in the stuffy, old house smelled stagnant and musty, so the first thing North did was walk from window to window, prying open the latches to let in some fresh air. The morning was already hot, pushing 90 degrees and definitely a day for the AC, but fortunately for her and the house, the breeze from Lake Michigan was crisp. Within minutes, the house was filled with fresh, clean air.

North took out an old t-shirt and began dusting the living room and first-floor master bedroom, which still contained a queen-sized bed and a pair of nightstands. After she cleaned all the surface areas, she gave both rooms a thorough vacuuming, making sure to get under any piece of furniture she couldn't move. Satisfied with her progress, she took the vacuum back to El's house and jumped online to order a bamboo sheet set, pillows, blanket, and a duvet for the bed, as well as a little something sexy for her to wear.

Later in the afternoon, North drove out to Filkins Vineyards, a nearby winery, which sat high on a hill and featured a large back deck overlooking the vineyards and the hills. North selected five pours that she thought might go well with whitefish, then she carried her tray of labeled wine glasses out to the back deck and took a seat in one of the Adirondack chairs that faced the vineyards. The wispy clouds were slowly rolling west, and she watched them, mesmerized, as she took sips of her wine, trying to imagine which wine would best complement an elegant fish dinner.

Sitting there, drinking good wine and soaking in the sun on a warm summer day, North let out a long sigh and realized that she felt more at peace than she had since "the day." She even toyed with the idea of talking to the winery owners about a part-time job, but then chuckled as she realized that working at a winery and visiting a winery are very different experiences. Working there just might destroy the sanctity of it all, and besides, after Friday, she might not be in the area any longer.

North took the last sip of her tasting and went back inside to select two bottles of chardonnay from the shelves for purchase and a very tasty dry Riesling. North thought that would be the perfect wine to open and make a toast to the house.

The rest of that day, along with the next, North found herself hyper-focused on shopping and getting the house ready for her first guest. It had to be perfect.

On Thursday, the topic for her radio show was all about embarrassing moments. It went fairly well, but it didn't have the same impact as the previous two shows. Drama always seems to get the high ratings, but North found it could also be draining. She thought it would be better for her and her audience if she mixed it up a bit by bringing a little lightness and laughter to it at least once a week.

It was finally Friday, and North could barely contain her excitement—not only was she looking forward to having some long-overdue sex with her husband, but she was also excited to show Matthew all of the work she had done on the stuffy, old house.

She drove out to Barden's Farm Market to find some local produce to go with her whitefish. She selected some green beans, a bunch of leaf lettuce, a red pepper, a red onion, and a quart of fresh strawberries. Satisfied with the freshness of her purchases, she drove back to the house and got to work.

It was a happy surprise for North that the house was stocked with all of its original kitchen implements. For whatever reason, the previous owners only took items that had personal value, leaving everything else to the new buyers. So, North had inherited some interesting pieces, including some very nice glass pie pans. She pulled one out of the cupboard, washed it, greased it, and set it aside so she could begin preparing the dough for the crust.

North spent the majority of the day in the kitchen creating a meal she knew Matthew would love. She prepared a flaky garlic and lemon butter-baked whitefish, fresh green beans with slivered almonds, a leaf lettuce salad with red onions and a sweet and tangy vinaigrette dressing (Matthew's mother's recipe), and the pièce de résistance—North's famous, mouthwatering strawberry pie. This one was her grandmother's recipe and Matthew would literally beg her to make it every time he brought a colleague over for dinner.

She set the table three times, first with china, fine linen napkins, and candles on a white tablecloth; but that was too obvious, so she pulled it all off and put out paper plates and plasticware, which made it look like she should be serving hot dogs and burgers. All she would need to complete that look was the bottle of ketchup, so she pulled everything off again and set out the white plates on the old wooden table with everyday silverware, and no centerpiece. That was the look—nice, but inconspicuous. It didn't feel like walking into an ambush. North cringed a little at that thought, but quickly convinced herself that tonight would be for the greater good for both of them.

Before she put the fish dish into the oven, North took her first shower in the old house. The bathroom had a certain charm, with its floral wallpaper and old ceramic faucet handles. She didn't know if they were original or not, but considered it a very nice touch. The bathroom floor was another story. The old, cracked tiles were edged by nearly black grout that, in many places, was chalky and rubbing away. She clenched her teeth as she covered the floor with towels to avoid stepping on it with her clean feet.

When her shower was finished, North dried herself off and creamed up her body with her favorite unscented lotion to which she'd added a few drops of Ysatis by Givenchy, which was Matthew's favorite perfume. Next, she put on a sundress she knew he loved—not too sexy, but it hugged her body in all the right places. It was just the right amount of sensual until the evening got hotter. Then, the naughty black lace bra and panties would seal the deal. She smiled as she dried her hair, lightly applied some foundation, liner, mascara, and lip gloss, and walked through one light spray of Ysatis to finish it all off.

Everything was set to go into the oven when Matthew's blue BMW pulled up the driveway.

With a deep breath, North said to herself, "Here we go girl. Time to fight for what's ours."

Chapter Nineteen

North felt butterflies in her stomach as she watched him get out of the car. He was dressed in khaki slacks with a loose-fitting white shirt, and his dark hair looked like it had been brushed to the side with his fingers. He was so handsome, he could have been a model.

Matthew caught her watching him from the kitchen doorway and flashed her a smile that created an instant warmth and tingling between her thighs. "He still owns me; dinner may just have to wait," she whispered to herself. Matthew then reached into the passenger seat and pulled out a gym bag.

North snickered, realizing that was what he used as an overnight bag. Always the practical one. He made great money, but he was never really extravagant with it, as if spending a little cash on a real piece of luggage could be considered extravagant.

She flung open the door. "Hey there. Welcome."

Matthew jumped up the two steps and gave her a quick hug. "Thank you." The gesture somehow felt awkward for both of them, and he moved on quickly.

"Tell you what," North said. "Let me get the food in the oven, and then I'll give you the little tour and tell you what I'm thinking."

"Sounds good." Matthew slung his gym bag over his shoulder and folded his arms while he waited. He was obviously nervous, which North thought would easily be remedied with a nice glass of wine.

North slid the pan of fish into the oven with the pan of green beans right below it, then closed the door, hit the timer, and grabbed the bottle of wine. "Let's get this celebration started. I have a special selection from Filkins Vineyards, a cute local winery not too far from here," she said. She uncorked the dry Riesling and poured it into two wine glasses that were a bit cloudy from age, but better than the red Solo cups she found stashed in the cupboard. She handed him a glass and held hers up. "To my first North Haven guest."

Matthew smiled. "Thanks. And to you, the unstoppable North Cooper."

They clinked glasses, and North smiled hearing Matthew use her married name. They both took healthy sips of the wine, and Matthew looked impressed. He held up the glass and inspected it. "This is really good, North. This is a Michigan wine?"

"Yep. The grapes are grown about twenty miles from here."

"Nice." He looked around at the rest of the house. "So how about that tour? I've never even seen the inside of this house before."

"Sure. Bring your wine with you." North took him out into the large foyer and discussed the office space that Brax had advised. Matthew agreed that it seemed like a good idea. "This is your new boyfriend you're talking about?"

North shook her head. "No, that's not working out."

"Oh, I'm sorry."

"Don't be," she said. Next, they leisurely wandered into the living room and discussed the changes and color scheme she had in mind.

North even surprised herself at how much thought she'd already invested into the decorating, as well as the detailed design plans she had in her head. Perhaps it would be wise for her to jot some of these down, just in case.

She walked back into the foyer, out to the large staircase. "There are six bedrooms upstairs, and then the third floor has smaller rooms that I could make into guest rooms and maybe charge a lesser rate. The view of Lake Michigan from up there is amazing. I have a feeling I may have guests requesting those rooms just to watch the sunsets."

"Good idea." Matthew followed along, intently listening to her every word. He seemed genuinely interested in what she had to say, even appearing as if he were impressed by her plans—perhaps even proud.

Matthew's encouragements had always been important to North. He had a way of making her feel as though she could do anything. She was holding on to his small bits of praise, like a child snatching M&Ms from her mother's generous hand.

"Finally, here is your room for the night." She led him into the master bedroom and gestured to the narrow wooden door off to the left. "And there is your en suite. Sorry, the towels drying in there are mine. I took a shower earlier, but I have others for you."

"Where are you sleeping?" Matthew asked.

"Oh, uhh," she stammered. She hadn't thought the question would come up. "I'm just going to sleep out on the sofa." She had planned to sleep in there with him, but it was too early into the evening to share that information.

Matthew shook his head. "Don't be silly. I'll take the couch."

"Oh, but I insist." North grabbed his gym bag off of his shoulder. "You can't be my first guest if you don't stay in the guest room." She set his bag on the bed, and a low sounding buzz was heard from the kitchen. "Tour's over just in time for dinner. C'mon." She took his hand and led him back out through the foyer and into the kitchen once more. "Finish your Riesling, I have another wine selection to pair with dinner."

Matthew did as he was told, tipping his glass all the way back and finishing the contents in one gulp.

North opened the oven and stepped back, letting the steam rise before grabbing the trays. The room filled with the savory aroma of lemon and garlic.

"Oh my," Matthew said, taking in a deep breath. "That smells incredible, and now my stomach's growling."

Pointing to the refrigerator with a hot pad, North said, "Could you please get the chardonnay out of the fridge and open it?"

North plated the food with as much finesse as a Michelin chef. The plates not only smelled delicious, but they also looked like they were set for a photo shoot. North knew she wasn't going to get Matt back with just good wine—she had to woo him through his stomach, too.

Matthew had the wine poured and was setting the glasses on the table when she walked over with the plates. Once they had taken their seats, he looked at her with a loving smile and held up his glass, saying, "To the prettiest B&B owner in South Haven."

North felt herself blush when she clinked his glass. It surprised her how much she needed to hear that, and that it came from the person she loved the most meant everything to her at that moment. Sipping their wine, they stared at each other with smiles. Then, Matthew set his glass down and focused on the food in front of him. He picked up his fork and took a small nibble out of the edge of the fish, closing his eyes and savoring it. He took another sip of wine to wash it down. "It's been so long since I've had one of your meals, that I forgot what a fantastic cook you are."

“Thanks,” North said, picking up her fork and tasting it herself. She had to admit; he was right. It was delicious. “So, tell me what’s going on in Ann Arbor. Are Jonah and Iris still hosting a dinner party every two to three weeks?”

“Oh my gosh,” Matthew chuckled. “They just don’t stop. And of course, Amit and I go separately as we’re still keeping our relationship on the down-low. I just don’t know how Jonah will react.”

This was the first North heard that Amit was back in the picture. “What do they say about us?” She wanted to stay off the topic of Amit.

Matthew sighed. “Iris asks about you every time I see her. Then she gives me this pitying look and shakes her head, like it’s the saddest thing imaginable that you and I aren’t together anymore.”

“Yeah. Well, how about work?” North said, realizing that leading off with friends and relationships was probably not the best tactic. “Any new interesting cases?”

“Oh, hell yeah.” Matthew said. “We had an older gentleman come in the other day presenting with weakness in his legs and an overall fatigue that seemed unnatural to him, even though he was 77 years old.” Matthew went on describing the interesting discoveries of that case, and then the one from the week before. North prodded him with questions to keep the conversation fluid. Talking made him thirsty, so she continued to fill up his wine glass each time it was half full. An hour later, she pulled out the strawberry pie and plated a piece with a healthy scoop of Hudsonville vanilla ice cream.

“Heaven on a plate,” Matthew said and devoured every last bite with several joyful “mmmm’s.”

The bottle of chardonnay was empty. Matthew had consumed the majority of it, and he was definitely feeling the effects.

North pulled the Riesling out of the refrigerator. "Why don't you grab your glass, and we'll head to the living room for a bit."

"Sounds good," said Matthew, wiping his mouth with his napkin and sliding his chair out. "Whoa," he said, placing a hand on the table to steady himself. "How much wine did I drink?"

North held up the bottle that was a little more than half full. "Not nearly enough. C'mon." She walked into the living room and nodded at the couch. "Have a seat."

Smiling, Matthew did as instructed.

North poured a healthy amount of wine into his waiting glass. "Did you make the Summer Festival this year?"

"Sadly, no." Matthew took a drink. "It seemed well-attended, though. Traffic was very heavy each day when I was getting out of work."

The Summer Festival was a big annual event in Ann Arbor featuring food, art, music, and even comedians. North had participated in it several times when she was with Michigan Radio, but it was also something she and Matthew liked to attend together. "How about the farmer's market?"

Trying to remain expressionless, Matthew shook his head, but his regret glistened in his cloudy eyes.

Another direct hit. She and Matthew would visit the farmer's market after he got out of work, slowly peruse the aisles, and then based upon the fresh options, decide what they were making for dinner. With local meats and fresh produce in hand, they would go home, turn on some music, and cook together. These were things she missed, and based on the look on his face, Matthew did, too.

"So, what have you been doing?"

Matthew shrugged and looked out the window. "Besides work, not much really." He turned his head and looked her in the eyes.

"Those things that we did together, they wouldn't be the same without you. I do miss those days, sometimes."

North spoke softly. "Me too."

North could see that the topics were awkward for him, as he took another long drink of wine to avoid continuing. He stretched, then rubbed his eyes. The wine was definitely going to his head.

"So, I have to ask," North wanted to keep some sort of conversation going. "What do you think of North Haven?"

"Oh," Matthew nodded enthusiastically, happy for the change in subject. "I'm very impressed, and I like your ideas. I'm just glad it's going to work out for you." He shifted his weight on the couch, and his hand shook a bit as he raised his glass. He took a quick sip, then brought his hand down, staring at his glass. "North, there is something I've wanted to talk to you about."

"Sure. What is it?"

Matthew took a steady deep breath before continuing. "Well, ahhh … we've been living apart now for quite a while, and … umm. Well, you're moving on with your life, and I'm moving on with mine. So, I think it may be time to start talking about …"

North's eyes widened. This was not the direction she wanted the conversation to go. She had wanted to wait until later, when candles were lit and the ambiance was much more romantic, but she didn't have the time. She set down her wine glass and lunged toward Matthew. She took his face in her hands and delivered one soft, lingering kiss. To her surprise, he didn't fight it. Her next kiss was firmer, and she let her tongue cautiously explore his hot, wet mouth. Like a hungry lion, Matthew leaned back and pulled her down on top of him, all the while kissing her like it was their last night on earth.

As their tongues danced together, North began quickly unbuttoning his shirt, and then lifted her dress over her head, revealing her ripe breasts adorned by black lace. She pulled back and gazed down at Matthew, who was looking up at her with eyes full of electricity and want. She was excited to see that look again and was ready to feed his lust. She stood up so he could view the black lace panties that completed the ensemble and take her all in.

His eyes opened wider as he caught his breath and looked her up and down. This was the reaction she was hoping for. North was feeling it as well, along with a sense of urgency to make love to her husband again. She smiled playfully at him through a lock of her long blonde hair and unfastened her bra, letting it fall to the floor.

Just as soon as her breasts were on full display a switch went off in Matthew. He took a quick breath, held up a hand, and said, "Wait, stop. This can't happen."

"But Matthew, it *is* happening," North said, and she laid back down on him again, rubbing his chest, kissing his neck while trying to take off his shirt.

"No, North," Matthew said. "I don't want this."

"Shhhh, don't say that." North wouldn't let up. She had been without the man she loved for so long, and she yearned for him now. If she wanted him this badly, she was sure he wanted her, too. She reached down, gently rubbed the front of his pants, and then unbuckled his belt.

"North. *No.*"

Matthew sat up and pushed her off of him.

North slid off the couch and bumped her head on the floor. She lay there, naked, looking up at the ceiling, feeling horrified, rejected, and humiliated. She crossed her arms to hide her breasts, rolled onto her side in the fetal position, and wept.

"I can't believe you did that!" Matthew shouted. "That was the most disrespectful thing you've ever done."

North clutched at her dress and pulled it over to cover herself. She put her other hand over her face, as if she could hide the fact that she was in tears.

Matthew jumped up from the couch. "I'm sorry," he said, as he stepped over her. "This is not me. I thought I made that clear to you."

"But it *was* you," North exclaimed. She pushed herself up on one hand, holding the dress over her with the other. "You were enjoying it. I saw it in your eyes."

"That's not what you saw." Matthew buttoned his shirt. "What you saw was nostalgia. What you saw was caring. What you saw was love." He tucked his shirt back into his pants. "I loved what we had, North, and I still love you, but I can't be that man anymore. I never was." He reached out to help her up off the floor.

North leaned away and shook her head.

Matthew pulled his hand back and stood tall. "I need to ask you something, and I need you to be honest with me. Was it your plan all along to bring me here, hypnotize me with food and wine, and then attempt to seduce me?"

North sniffed, wiped at her tears, and said nothing.

"It was, wasn't it?" Matthew said.

North took a breath. "I just thought …" she wiped at her running nose, "that if we were to make love, you'd remember that what we had was really special, and …"

Matthew huffed and walked off in the direction of the bedroom. He returned a moment later with his gym bag slung over his shoulder.

"No, Matthew. You don't have to go," North said. "I'll go. I don't want you to drive. You've been drinking."

Matthew shook his head. "I'll be fine." He looked at her with an expression North had never seen before. There was contempt in his eyes. Disappointment. Disgust. "Look North," he said softly, but with conviction. "I loved you, not because of the great sex, but because you were a genuinely kind person and a great example of humanity. You have a heart like nobody I've ever met, and even when I realized who I truly am, you were still so important and special to me that I would have done anything to keep you a part of my life. But after this, I realize it's not possible."

North couldn't hold back her anguish anymore. She sat on the floor with her back to the couch, burying her face in her hands, and wailed like a wounded animal.

Matthew, unfazed by her tears, continued in his cold, bitter tone. "You said you had hooked up with someone. You made it seem like you were moving on. I don't know if that was a lie to put me at ease and lower my guard, or if you really did do it, but it got me here. I actually came to talk about the divorce. I thought it might be a good time, now that you seemed to be moving forward with your life. But then ..." he gestured toward the couch. After a short pause and a glare of disdain he continued. "I now realize I can't worry about it any longer. I've put my own life off long enough. You can expect to be served with divorce papers within the week." He turned and walked toward the kitchen.

North twirled up on her knees. "Matthew, don't go. I'm sorry."

Matthew paused in the foyer. He glanced back over his shoulder and said sadly, "Goodbye North." Then he hurried on out through the kitchen.

North heard the screen door squeak open, then swing closed with a clack. She crawled up on the couch and collapsed onto her side. When she heard his BMW start up and drive off, she broke into an uncontrollable fit of crying. Her tears soaked into the velour fabric of the old sofa.

When she was all cried out, she took deep breaths and laid there for another hour in silence. The house seemed so big now. So harsh. So foreign.

And North felt nothing but alone.

Chapter Twenty

Not wanting to stay in that old lonely house all night, North drove home and quietly slipped into her room. She heard the low muffle of the TV on in the living room, and realized she didn't feel like being alone, either. She crept out into the hall to find the house smelled of fresh baked bread. It was warm and inviting.

It was home.

Tiptoeing to the end of the hallway, North peered around the corner and saw Aunt El watching one of the Real Housewives shows. She had always called them her guilty pleasure. "All those people with all that money, and not a single one of them is actually happy."

El sat there, so content with life, playing Mahjong on her phone while the wealthy ladies on TV constantly complained about each other. Every once in a while, El would chuckle and shake her head.

North didn't really care for the Real Housewives, but she didn't want to be alone right then, so she walked out and sat down on the flowered sofa.

"Good Lord, North, you gave me a fright!" Aunt El grabbed the remote, hit the mute button and looked into her eyes. "Why, you've been crying. What's wrong, honey?"

"I don't think I can talk about it." North wiped at her eyes as the tears started to well up again.

El put down her phone, turned off the TV, and sat on the sofa next to North. "Come on, child. Tell me all about it."

North leaned her head on the old woman's shoulder and felt an instant calm. She let her body relax and allowed herself to enjoy the mothering she'd never really had growing up. It was several minutes before she could bring herself to say a word, and El gave her all the time she needed by holding her hand and gently patting her knee.

Slowly, North began to talk. She told El how excited she was that Matthew was coming to see the house; she talked about how she cleaned, shopped, and prepared all the food for his visit; she even shared how she selected the wines for the evening and the intimate details about her mission to get Matthew loosened up to seduce him. She wept as she explained how everything blew up in her face and ruined what could have been, should have been, a beautiful evening.

"North, I just don't understand. Why on earth would you ever try to seduce him?"

North rubbed at her eyes once more. "I just knew that if we could connect again, he would remember how much he loved me and that we are meant to be together."

El tapped her knee. "Look at me, girl."

North lifted her weary head.

El grabbed both of her shoulders and turned her face to look directly into her eyes. "My dear, I know this is very difficult for you. You seem to believe that you may have done something wrong—that your actions may have caused him to give up women." She shook her head. "It just doesn't work that way, and through all this muck,

Matthew has treated you with so much kindness since he has come out. You have to appreciate that. You have to appreciate the fact that you have a dear friend in him, but most importantly, you have got to understand that your marriage is done. That life is behind you. If you continue down this path of desperation, you will end up being the villain of your own story, and you'll be miserable the rest of your life."

North dropped her head and gasped at the air, trying not to completely break down.

"I know. I know." Aunt El pulled her in close and held her tight, her whole body shaking, gently rocking her back and forth. She didn't try to make another point or say another word. Instead, she simply whispered, "That's alright. Get it out, dear girl," and, "You're gonna be fine. I'm here, and I ain't leaving you."

Eventually, North's tears ran out, and she was exhausted. El guided her off the sofa and into her room. "You get yourself into bed, and I'll be right back."

Pulling off her shirt and shorts, North slid into the cool covers. She laid there, staring at the ceiling, wondering what her life was going to be now. It was as if she had rewound two months. She allowed herself to believe that she could convince Matthew that he was not gay. Not for one second, in all her planning, did she consider how ridiculous that was. "You're such an idiot," she thought. North closed her eyes and draped her arm over her face.

"There will be no negative self-talk, my dear," Aunt El said.

North peered out from under her arm just as El arrived on the edge of the bed holding a bowl with a spoon. "I have for you a surefire mood fixer."

North scooted herself up to see El proudly handing her a bowl of fresh, juicy strawberries dripping over one of El's scratch-made biscuits with a dollop of whipped cream on top.

The first taste made her believe Aunt El was right. The biscuit was warm and comforting. Much of it had soaked in the fresh, semi-tart juices of the strawberries, and combined with the sweetness of the whipped cream, it was a perfect bite.

She took her time savoring each bite of the dessert, eating as if it were her last meal upon this earth. She even scraped the last soggy crumbs out of the bottom.

El chuckled and took the bowl from her. "Does the world feel a little better now?"

North nodded and slid back under the covers.

Aunt El set the bowl down on the nightstand and tucked her in, whispering in her ear, "There's more out there to make sure you have a better day tomorrow. Mark my words, you will, and it will continue to get better with each passing day." El kissed her on the forehead and said, "Now try and get some sleep, sweet girl, so that the better days can begin."

Grabbing the bowl, El walked out of the room, flipping the switch and closing the door, leaving North in the fading light of day from cracks around the window shades.

After a day filled with so much emotion, North found that sleep came easier than she expected.

North felt emotionally hungover and spent Saturday sitting in the backyard in shorts, an oversized t-shirt, and a ball cap. She had neither the desire nor the energy to even walk down to the beach. She simply sat and replayed the painful events of the previous evening, recalling the look on Matthew's face when he'd said, "I don't want this."

She closed her eyes and shook her head at the thought.

How many times had it been said that no means no? It goes both ways, but why hadn't she listened when Matthew said no?

Aunt El was right. North was becoming the villain of her own story, and she felt nothing but shame. It was hard to get excited about life when you didn't even like what you'd become.

Unfortunately, she had to pull herself together for her shift on Sunday evening. She showered, put on clean sweats, and headed down to the station, wondering just how she was going to make it through a show.

"Hey, North—you doing okay?" Li asked her.

North sat down, shook her head, and began her prep work, adding songs and commercial spots to the computer playlist.

"Anything I can do?"

Again, North shook her head.

"Okay … well … I hope things get better. Have a good show." Li gathered her things and quietly left the building.

North put her headphones on and waited for George Michael to finish singing "Faith." Then, instead of playing Marcus's pre-produced intro, she just turned on her mic. "Hey South Haven, this is North Nichols, I hope you're having a good Sunday. The other day, someone I love and respect very much told me that I was becoming the villain of my own story. I don't think her words hurt as much as the realization that she was absolutely right. I won't go into the sordid details, but suffice to say, I messed up big time, and it's hard to forgive myself.

"So, I ask you: Has there ever been a time when you were the villain of your own story? What did you do, and how were you able to finally move forward afterwards?"

Even before North had finished her questions, the studio telephone lines were lighting up. For the next hour, she moderated stories about cheating husbands, cheating wives, keying cars, and flattening tires. One woman even admitted to spray-painting four-letter words all over her ex-boyfriend's new truck, and another caller admitted to poisoning the neighbor's dog that had bitten his then-six-year-old son.

"Okay," North said, firmly. "I'm not talking about criminal acts, here. I'm asking about a time when you experienced tunnel vision and felt driven to do something to fulfill some selfish need, but hurt someone you cared about in the process. Maya Angelou said, 'When you know better, you do better.' But there is no, 'When you know better, you get to rewind the clock and have a redo.' Some mistakes are ugly, and second chances are a luxury few of us get. How do you move on, knowing that the someone you hurt may never forgive you?"

The new twist North had added quickly dimmed the lights on the studio lines. The consensus seemed to be that if people felt justified in what they were doing, they had little concern for what others thought or felt. She ended up playing more music than she had planned. Sitting alone in the studio, listening to OneRepublic sing "Apologize" with the words, "It's too late to apologize," nearly brought her to tears.

One woman called and talked about her husband, who was emotionally and verbally abusive. For years she'd dealt with it, hoping he would mellow, but he never did. Her biggest ally was her husband's brother, who had always been kind and quick to defend her. They eventually ended up having an affair. Years later, when the affair was discovered, it not only created a war between the brothers, but the whole family got involved, destroying many bonds. The woman not only felt bad about it, but she was also carrying a tremendous amount of guilt because she truly loved her husband's family. They had always treated her kindly, and it was never her intention to hurt any of them.

North thought the audience would appreciate the woman's story, but there was also the fact that she could be considered justified in her actions because she had been abused. It didn't quite correlate to what North had done. She had no excuses. She *was* a villain.

A little later in the evening, a woman called in with a story North needed to hear. "You're on True North. Do you have a story where you're the villain?"

"I suppose so," the woman said tentatively. "At least several people think so, or they think I'm a joke."

"Talk to me," North said.

"Well, I married my high school sweetheart, but when we graduated, we made plans to go off to college. We both started at Lansing Community College, because that was the area we were both from. After we finished our programs, he transferred to Michigan State University, where we lived in the married housing section while I got a job to support us. He was going for his undergraduate degree in finance, and after he completed it, I had planned to go back for a degree in theater to become an actress. This was no secret. He had known of my aspirations since high school—I had even been in all of the school musicals and usually got the lead role. Acting was not just my dream; it was my passion. Once my husband graduated from MSU and entered his career field, I told him it was my turn to go back to school to pursue my theater degree. My instructor at LCC helped me obtain a scholarship to CMU for musical theater, but the challenge was that I would have to live on campus because it was too far of a daily commute. Despite the fact it was mostly paid for, my husband stated in no uncertain terms that if I were to pursue it, we were done. He would file for divorce and our marriage would be over. So I gave up the scholarship and the opportunity to pursue my dream. I settled for the only job I could get and worked full-time as a bank teller for years. Later, we were blessed with three children, whom I love very much. Eventually, my husband was promoted to a higher position and gained a salary that more than covered all our expenses. Since I no longer needed to work, I quit my job and became more involved in the lives of my kids. I became the mom who volunteered in the classroom, chaperoned field trips, and made treats for the class. I also became the wife who hosted last-minute dinner parties and extravagant holiday parties for his colleagues and friends. Don't get me wrong, I love them very much, and I loved being a wife and mother, but I never gave up my dream of acting. Whenever I brought up the idea of community theater, my husband would become angry. He felt I needed to be there for the kids, and just what would all of our friends think? Ultimately, the kids grew up and went off to college, and we had a service come in to clean the house. There really wasn't anything left for me to do. So, one day I snapped and made the bold decision to put myself first. I left the marriage to finally pursue my own dream. My husband and my children were all very upset with me, and even broke off all contact for a period of time."

"That's awful," North said.

"It was very difficult, but I wasn't going to be deterred. This was basically my last shot to follow my dream, and I was committed. I am now acting at the Grand Rapids Civic Theatre and School of Theatre Arts. It's one of the largest community theaters in the U.S., and everyone there is very encouraging. All of our old mutual friends chose him over me, but that's okay. I have a new tribe now, and friends who are warm, kind, and encouraging. I get up every morning excited about the day. I truly love what I do, and I've even had a couple good reviews. Best of all, all three of my kids have forgiven me and regularly attend my plays."

"Wow," North said. "You've been practicing for this role your entire life."

"What?" asked the woman. "What do you mean?"

"You have been *acting* like the happy wife and the happy mother. You have been *acting* like you were fulfilled. You had something in your soul that was calling you, pulling you to another kind of life, yet you have been acting like you had no dreams. You were an Oscar winner on the stage of life. It's no wonder you're excelling at it now."

"Hmmm, I didn't think of that. I guess you're right."

"Thank you for sharing, and best of luck with your new career and your new life." North hit the button to play the next song and turned off her mic.

The last caller had done it. She helped North realize what she had been missing—what El had been telling her from the first day they were reunited. While North listened to this woman pour out her life-long struggle, she'd realized that Matthew had been doing the *exact* same thing. Matthew had been acting like the loving husband, even though his heart, his mind, his whole soul, was telling him that North was not the right person for him.

The question is, why would he do that? Why would he pretend to be something he was not for so long?

Why did the female caller pretend to be a happy wife and mother for so long? She had answered that question: because she had three kids that she loved very much and that needed her.

Perhaps Matthew felt she needed him.

Matthew had given North some of the best years of his life. He had taken very good care of her then, and he was still trying to take care of her. Buying her a house that she could turn into a profitable business is a very caring act.

Even though he claimed to love her very much, he wasn't capable of continuing the charade of being the man she needed him to be. This was a light bulb moment for North. She blinked her eyes as she realized the real reason he reacted so harshly when she attempted to make love to him. It wasn't because he found her disgusting, but because he saw the act as a bridge that, if crossed, would mean the end of his opportunity to live the life he was meant for.

He would be betraying *himself*.

North sighed and dropped her head into her hands. This epiphany had come with the awful realization that Aunt El was right. North was wrong to be angry with Matthew for "turning" gay. Nobody *turns* gay. She realized the root of her anger had more to do with her own selfish concern about what she would be losing, rather than tapping into her compassion for Matthew and what he had given up while they'd been together.

Was it possible that Emma knew all along that her brother was gay? Perhaps that was why she'd judged North's reaction so harshly. Could it be that she understood how difficult it was for Matthew to come out like he did?

It was as though the dark clouds parted and the sun, shining brightly, cast beams of light on all the things she needed to see.

North took a long drink from her water bottle, finished up the show, then left and walked down to the end of the pier. She leaned against the lighthouse and listened to the water lapping against the rocks and the cries of the gulls on the beach. She watched the light of magic hour slowly cede to the night and realized she didn't want another day to end on a sour note. She felt a surge of energy run through her, and with it, the urgent desire to begin taking steps to improve her life and the lives of those she cared about.

North pulled out her phone and hit Matthew's number. As she suspected, he didn't answer, but she knew the words she needed to say. "Hey Matthew," she began. "I just wanted to call to say a few things. Tonight, a woman called into my radio show and shared an interesting story. I won't go into everything she said, but basically, she lived the first half of her life for everyone else. She continuously put herself last, until one day she couldn't do it anymore. As I listened to her, I realized that's what you had been doing for me. I can't begin to tell you how sorry I am for the other night. I hope, in time, you will find it in your heart to forgive me. Anyway, please know that I will sign the divorce papers as soon as I receive them. I want to help you to move forward with the life you've waited so long to live in any way I can. Take care, Matthew."

She hung up the phone feeling lighter, as though she had just thrown a weighted blanket off her, and she could breathe again. Her stomach was filled with a mix of fear and excitement. North felt that was exactly as it should be. She looked up at the sky to see night rolling in and saw millions of twinkling stars populating the indigo sky. Her biggest wish at the moment was that Matthew would find a way to forgive her and continue to be some small part of her life, but that would have to be his decision, and she would no longer try to influence it. If he needed to distance himself from her, she would accept that and move on.

At that moment, her phone buzzed in her hand, and she looked down to see she had a text from Matthew. He had sent her one single red heart.

Chapter Twenty-One

Whether it was a coincidence, or just some energy in the universe, the very show that had made all the difference in her personal life had also made all the difference in her ratings.

Marcus was thrilled, because her show began to bring in a lot of advertising revenue. Wisely, he invested the unexpected windfall by expanding the promotions for her show as far north as Grand Haven and as far south as New Buffalo. Additionally, he began making improvements around the station—a fresh coat of paint, more comfortable studio chairs, and two vending machines for drinks and snacks (which they all decided was the best improvement yet).

It wasn't long before North began receiving more calls than she could handle. She was also getting a fair amount of prank calls, which annoyed her, but absolutely enraged Marcus. To mitigate it, he began staying on as her producer, screening all calls before they got to her. Later, he invested in the most impactful improvement of all: he had the small storage room next to the studio converted into a producer's studio, complete with a large window in the wall, so producer and host could see each other as the calls were coming in.

Once that was complete, Marcus hired a young woman who'd just graduated from Lake Michigan Community College as North's producer. Her name was Laura, and she and North hit it off immediately.

North let Dietra LaRue-Perkins know that she would be keeping the house, though she tried to soften the blow by bringing her a bottle of chardonnay from Filkins Vineyards. "I'd really appreciate any advice you could give me to help make it successful."

Dietra glared at her, reached out to grab the wine, and then closed the door with a slam.

North moved on and hired a new contractor that wouldn't be a distraction or a temptation. Her name was Deb Dunfoy, a cute, petite brunette in her mid-forties. Her business was called, "Dunfoy and Daughters," and she had two twenty-something daughters, Jordan, who had bright red hair, always braided, and Jemma, a strawberry-blonde cross-fitter who could lift more weight than most men.

Deb and her daughters had been struggling to get their contracting business off the ground simply because of their genders, but this intrigued North. She requested to see photos of their previous work, which included a kitchen remodel for a relative, a bathroom remodel for a friend. The job that sold North, however, was a treehouse—or perhaps the better term was a tree-mansion—for a paying client. The ladies had completed a little over a dozen projects, but nothing as big as what North was proposing. They were so interested in the job, they even reduced their bid to make it more appealing. However, North had plans to pay them full price if everything turned out as they promised.

The divorce process was draining, and although North tried to make it as amicable as possible, Matthew's disposition was cold and unpleasant. He said he forgave her for the "failed seduction," but he was emotionally distant and barely polite. She didn't blame him, and she accepted her role in their fractured relationship.

The divorce proceedings seemed set up to be combative. They

were placed in a sterile conference room in Ann Arbor, Matthew and his Armani-clad lawyer, Edward, on one side of the table, and her lawyer, a young black woman named Rhoda, just one year out of law school, on the other side. What she didn't have in experience, she made up for in tenacity.

Edward argued that since Matthew had already purchased a house for North, retribution had been satisfied. Rhoda, however, argued that it was a gift presented during the marriage, and the value was not to be considered in determining alimony. Furthermore, since the couple was married during the time Matthew attended medical school, North was entitled to half of his retirement income. Matthew's attorney became indignant over that request, which North believed was all just posturing, as it was not unheard of in the sector of divorce to consider retirement incomes.

Though Matthew rarely looked at her, North watched him morph into something she barely recognized during the settlement meeting. He seemed to be getting swept up in the contentiousness of it all. She observed how he glared at Rhoda, and she noticed how every time she spoke, his face would grow a deeper shade of red, contorting angrily.

This all had to end, and end quickly. The lawyers were not concerned with what the post-divorce relationship would look like, but it mattered very much to North. She had come to terms with the fact that Matthew wasn't going to be her husband, but she had no desire for him to become her archenemy. She stood up, slapped her hand on the table and called out, "Point of order." She didn't know if it was appropriate or not, but it was always effective on the various legal shows she liked to watch. Everyone stopped talking and looked at her. She pressed her lips tightly together, held up a finger, and said, "I need a five-minute recess to chat with my lawyer."

Once they left the room, North looked directly into her attorney's eyes and said, "I'm done. The house is more than enough, and I don't want a penny of his retirement. I'm pretty sure you may see this as reckless, and perhaps it is, but the one thing I'm sure of is that a future friendship with him is more important to me than any amount of money."

In the end, Matthew looked relieved to be finished with the arguing and viewed her actions as a generous olive branch. His demeanor softened, and she caught a glimpse of the old Matthew when he met her halfway by proposing a modest alimony. North was grateful, but Rhoda acted like she lost. What her youth, or perhaps her career choice hadn't made her aware of was that some things were worth more than money. Matthew was a truly good man and sometimes just having a good person in your corner, in any capacity, could make you emotionally wealthy. What could be more of a win than that?

It was in the middle of a hot August day a few weeks later that she found herself back in Ann Arbor headed to Matthew's house to sign the final divorce agreement. He had suggested that the papers be sent to her in South Haven, but she wanted to sign them with him to create a symbolic moment—a moment where their relationship transformed into something new, rather than the breaking of a dream.

She pulled her Subaru into the driveway of the brick house she had once called home. It felt different to her now. What had once seemed charming and idyllic, now felt isolated and foreign. North's life had changed more than she'd realized. In her present life, she now sat in a radio studio with a window that faced Lake Michigan. She was able to look out at the endless horizon, at least on the days when she could see past the crush of tourists, and she felt a new sense of freedom. The landscape was open, the air swirled in fresh and clean off the water, and the end of each day was punctuated with its own unique, spectacular sunset. But here, in the familiar wooded hills of Fair Oaks, she now felt cut off from the world.

She got out of her car and saw Amit's red BMW in the garage.

Had Matthew called him over for moral support or was this just a part of his daily routine?

North smiled at the irony of it all. Not long ago, she had been dreading this day. The very thought of it shot her anxiety level, normally at a two, straight to a ten, but ever since the day she had the epiphany about Matthew during her radio show, everything had changed. The chains of fear, self-pity, and despair became clear, as did her power to break them, just by changing her attitude.

The moment she made the choice to shift her thoughts, the most amazing things happened: the chains fell, the fog of her fear lifted, and the only things left in sight were possibilities.

After taking a deep, cleansing breath, she made another choice. She decided not to enter the house through the garage as she had in the past, opting instead to go to the front door and ring the bell like a proper guest.

Matthew opened the door. "Why didn't you just come in through the garage?"

"I just wanted to begin our new chapter with respect to boundaries," she said with a shrug and a smile.

He smiled back and gestured toward the kitchen. "Well, thank you. Come on in."

Stepping inside, North noticed the place hadn't changed much, not that she'd expected it would. She had been the designer in the family, not Matthew.

"This way," Matthew said. He was stiff and nervous.

North followed him into the kitchen to find Amit sitting at the same counter where he had been the first time she encountered this man in her home. He gave her a nervous smile, a slight nod, and lifted his fingers off the countertop just enough to suffice as a wave.

A manila folder filled with papers sat on the edge of the counter with a black pen resting expectantly on top. The energy in the house was heavy and uncomfortable, and North was not up to participating like this. She had learned that if people expected something to be painful and hard, then it would definitely end up that way. She had also learned that when you view things from a different perspective, you might be able to defy your original expectations.

With that in mind, she headed straight to the refrigerator and opened it up. Sure enough, there was a bottle of wine chilling right where she had left it several months before. It was a dry Riesling from Chateau Aeronautique, a winery located just outside of Jackson that she loved to visit with Matthew.

"What are you doing?" Matthew asked.

"This is a big moment for the three of us, right?" North said, grabbing the corkscrew and plunging it down into the cork.

Matthew and Amit glanced at each other but said nothing.

"I think it's only fitting that we treat it like a big moment," she added. She pulled the handles, and the cork popped free. "Isn't that a great sound?" she said with a laugh. "Matthew, could you please get us some glasses?"

Matthew glanced over at Amit again and pulled three glasses off the rack, setting them awkwardly on the counter with shaking hands.

North realized he wasn't going to relax until the papers were signed. "Okay, let's let that breathe a moment while we take care of business." She pointed to the folder, saying, "Amit, would you please slide that over here?"

With eyebrows raised, Amit gazed at her and slid the folder slowly with two fingers, as if it might burn him.

North picked up the pen, opened the folder, turned to the last page of the packet, then signed and dated it. She closed the folder, slid it over to Matthew, and turned her attention back to the wine.

"Okay. It's breathed enough. Want to hear another great sound?" She picked up the bottle and tipped it. It softly glugged as the first glass was poured. "Is there a happier sound on the planet?" she asked, sliding the glass in front of Matthew, who stood there with his arms crossed.

Both men smiled nervously.

The second glass, she slid in front of Amit. When she'd finished pouring her own glass, she picked it up, swirled it around, then put her nose down into the glass and inhaled. "Ahh, now that's a lovely bouquet." With a smile, North looked up and spoke softly. "Amit, I want to share something about the man you're getting involved with." Both men looked at each other, then back at her, not knowing what to expect. "He is one of the sweetest, kindest, most generous, and caring individuals I've ever known. The years we spent together were some of the happiest of my life. My wish for you, moving forward from today, is that he makes your life as wonderful as he made mine." She held up her glass. "To many years of happiness for the both of you."

Amit and Matthew looked at each other again, mouths hanging slightly ajar, then they each picked up their glasses and looked into them, as if she might have poisoned them.

"Are you guys going to leave me hanging here? That was a pretty damn good toast, if I do say so myself."

They chuckled and clinked her glass, then sipped their wine, smiling at each other.

"One more thing," North said.

They both looked at her like this was the moment they had anticipated.

"He snores like a wildebeest, so good luck with that," she said with a wink.

They both laughed, and Amit said, "That's putting it mildly."

North nearly spit out her wine, she was laughing so hard.

Matthew relaxed, and pulled out some cheese, olives, salami, and crackers, and quickly threw together a charcuterie board to enjoy while they drank their wine.

The next hour was spent at the counter, talking and laughing.

"I really like your radio show," Matthew admitted. "You do a great job."

"You get it clearly over here?" North asked.

"He listens to it on the internet," Amit said. "In fact, he never misses it. I like it, too. The topics you discuss are very interesting."

"Thank you." After spending some time with Amit, North could finally understand why Matthew was drawn to him. He had a certain exotic charm and oozed with both intelligence and wit.

When the bottle was finished, North stood and grabbed her purse. "Well, this has been really fun, but I need to get going. I have quite a drive ahead of me."

"Are you sure you're good to drive?" Matthew said. "You're welcome to stay here tonight."

"Thank you, but I'm good. I only drank two glasses." She smiled at the thought that he still cared about her safety.

She gave each of them a quick hug, then headed home, delighted that the whole event went better than she'd expected.

For the sake of nostalgia, she took the scenic back roads home, the way she and Matthew used to go when heading out on one of their long weekends. It seemed like a lifetime ago. It was strange to think how much her life had changed in just five short months. She now felt more confident than she ever had, and more importantly, she'd learned to be excited about the uncertainties in her life, rather than terrified. Uncertainty now meant an undiscovered opportunity, and not some monster lurking behind a corner.

Singing along with the radio at the top of her lungs, North was just fifteen miles from South Haven when a sign caught her eye. She wasn't sure she'd read it right, so she pulled into the driveway of a farm and turned around. She drove up to the billboard and couldn't believe her eyes, so she spun her car around in a perfect U-turn and pulled off to the side of the road.

Looking to make sure no traffic was coming, North stepped out of her car, walked around, and looked up at the billboard that had her photo plastered on it, larger than life. Her eyes opened wide with surprise, and she stood there frozen. She remembered the day that Marcus had come in and taken it. She had been sitting in the studio with her hair slightly messed up, because she had just pulled her headphones off. The words read, *"Find True North, weeknights at 6:00 on WSHS."*

North shook her head and laughed out loud. The past few months she had been stumbling through, just trying to put one foot in front of the other and survive her roller coaster of emotions. Yet in that time, she had managed to make something of herself. She knew the show had probably been more of a lifeline for her than to any of her listeners. She was definitely not an expert in human behavior, but perhaps that was the reason people tuned in. They weren't interested in hearing what an expert had to say; they were simply listening for perspective from anyone who was willing to call in and share. It seemed to North that the listeners were mainly just looking to be heard, and perhaps, to connect.

Whatever the reasons, her face on this sign was validation that North had found her place in the world. Her tribe. She was now part of a community where she felt appreciated.

Honestly, she had never felt better about herself than at that very moment.

North let a tear roll down her cheek, gave herself a hug, and smiled at the billboard that hundreds of people would drive by every day.

She climbed back into her car and headed … home.

Author's Note

First impressions are extremely important, so let me begin by thanking the people responsible for the first impression of this book—Kevin Fowler and his incredible photography work, and Jen Hayes, the model in the cover image. I have had many compliments about the cover so I wanted to direct those to the two individuals who truly deserve it.

Dayna on her deck in Michigan writing.

You may not be aware, but this book means more to me than any book I have written or intend to write in the future. It is the only book I will ever have the opportunity to write with my writing partner, and my life partner, Dayna Marie.

When I explained this to the remarkable folks at Mission Point Press they understood immediately and treated the book with the utmost care and attention. I have an incredible amount of gratitude to the team at MPP, especially those I have had direct contact with, including Jen Wahi, Tamra Tuller, Michelle DiMercurio, and the amazing editing job of Anna Faller.

I am actually writing because Dayna encouraged/demanded I do so. She never stopped telling me I was a good storyteller and was so relentless in her message she made me believe it myself, and I actually joined the local writing community.

Dayna was always my writing partner. She loved to discuss ideas for new stories, and creating characters together was a favorite pastime of hers. There were times we would get wine and snacks and sit out on the deck and spend hours creating lives, backstories, tics and quirks for all of the characters of the latest book I was writing. And then I would read her each chapter after it was written. I always felt her input was spot on and invaluable.

Then came the day I bounced an idea off her. I thought it might be cool to create a character in a small town in Michigan, that an audience could care for, and that we could perhaps have more than one book about. Perhaps even a series. I brought up the name "Joan of Arcadia" (because there is a small town in Michigan named Arcadia) but I knew that was already a Disney thing so we couldn't' use that. I didn't know that the idea struck such a chord with her, but a week or so later she called me at work and asked if I remembered bringing up the story about the person in Michigan (the number of story ideas I never wrote down and have since lost is countless at this point). When I told her that I did, she hit me with "North of South Haven." She had lived in South Haven as a child and had taken me to that idyllic coastal town several times to show me all the wonderful things she remembered as a child. I knew immediately that I wanted to do the book and I wanted her to write it with me. She was hesitant about the writing part, but I convinced her we could make it work and she finally agreed.

Then came hours of walking and hiking through Michigan woods and trails while we hashed out the story and the characters. North

Nichols was everything from a Hollywood star returning to her roots, to a New York financier coming back to South Haven to heal after a tragic car accident.

Though not in any way biographical, the book is peppered with people and moments from Dayna's past. Even the name of the character Eljerita came from a mysterious woman who appeared out of nowhere to help Dayna with a stressful moment with her kids when they were very young and then disappeared as quickly as she appeared. Dayna never forgot her and wanted to show her some love.

Thought there isn't an actual radio station in South Haven, Dayna had an extensive radio background and so it made sense to include that as a strength of North's. It also gave us a way to help North's character arc. Though Aunt El told North everything she needed to know to grow, we never listen to the people closest to us and North learned many of her life lessons from callers on her show.

When it came time to do the actual writing, Dayna was intimidated by the empty page, so I would write the framework of each chapter, and she would come back through and add the flavor. Much like I was the play-by-play and she was the color commentator. Then we would read each chapter back together, pick it apart and improve it together. There was a lot of trust involved, but that wasn't difficult as we were each other's biggest fan! It was the single most rewarding and enjoyable writing experiences I have ever had.

Years before, Dayna had been diagnosed with Chronic Lymphocytic Leukemia and as we were getting started with the book it really began affecting her health. She was going through chemotherapy at the time, and when she was recovering, I would work several chapters ahead, and then she would catch up when her health improved.

We actually finished the book the summer of 2023 but didn't really do anything with it because we had so much more to do together before she left (we knew there was no cure and that she would be moving on soon). We had ideas and storylines for more North of South Haven books but that will not happen now.

Dayna Marie passed away in February of 2024. I will never stop loving her or missing her, but I look back at this experience (just one of many) that we shared, and consider it an amazing gift that a very few get to have together. And her words will forever live on in this book. We were married later in life, and always joked that North was the daughter that we had together. That is why it will never be outdone as the most important book I have ever worked on.

We hope you enjoyed it.

About the Authors

Anybody who met Dayna Marie Edwards remembers her as the sweetest person, the brightest light, and the kindest heart they ever knew. Dayna had experience in a variety of industries, from medical assisting, to banking, to helping run a plumbing company. But her true passion was in media. She was the face in many commercials and a voice on two radio stations in the Lansing area. After earning her master's degree in communications, she was hired to start a media department within a Fortune 500 company. What she never let on was that she was a very talented poet and writer. After encouraging her husband to tell his stories, she came up with one of her own that they wrote together.

Very sadly she lost her long battle with chronic lymphocytic leukemia in 2024, but her dream and her words live on in North of South Haven, and those lives she touched throughout her life will forever miss her.

The majority of Rob Edwards's working life has been in the video and film production world, giving him ample experience with storytelling and the creative process. He has written throughout his career, and has won national and international awards for his work.

He is now transforming his efforts to the page, rather than the screen.

www.ingramcontent.com/pod-product-compliance
Lightning Source LLC
Chambersburg PA
CBHW030916060726
47591CB00005B/1563

* 9 7 8 1 9 6 8 7 6 1 3 6 3 *